Vanished

McIntyre Security Bodyguard Series

Book 15

by

April Wilson

Copyright © 2023 April E. Barnswell/
Wilson Publishing LLC
All rights reserved.

Proofreading by Sherry Fowler-Schafer, Lori Holmes, and Adelle Medhi

Cover by Steamy Designs
Photography by Reggie Deanching
Model: Robert Kelly

Published by
April E. Barnswell
Wilson Publishing LLC
P.O. Box 292913
Dayton, OH 45429
www.aprilwilsonauthor.com

ISBN: 9798385777907

No part of this publication may be reproduced, stored in a retrieval system, copied, shared, or transmitted in any form or by any means without the prior written permission of the author. The only exception is brief quotations to be used in book reviews. Please don't steal e-books.

This novel is entirely a work of fiction. All places and locations are used fictitiously. The names of characters and places are figments of the author's imagination, and any resemblance to real people or real places is purely coincidental and unintended.

Books by April Wilson

McIntyre Security Bodyguard Series:
Vulnerable
Fearless
Shane–a novella
Broken
Shattered
Imperfect
Ruined
Hostage
Redeemed
Marry Me–a novella
Snowbound–a novella
Regret
With This Ring–a novella
Collateral Damage
Special Delivery
Vanished

McIntyre Security Bodyguard Series Box Sets:
Box Set 1
Box Set 2
Box Set 3
Box Set 4

McIntyre Security Protectors:
Finding Layla
Damaged Goods
Freeing Ruby

McIntyre Search and Rescue:
Search and Rescue
Lost and Found
Tattered and Torn

Tyler Jamison Novels:
Somebody to Love
Somebody to Hold
Somebody to Cherish

A British Billionaire Romance Series:
Charmed
Captivated

Miscellaneous Books:
Falling for His Bodyguard

* * *

Audiobooks by April Wilson
For links to my audiobooks, please visit my website:
www.aprilwilsonauthor.com/audiobooks

Character List

Main Characters

- Sophie McIntyre Zaretti – 33 yrs old, interior designer, married to Dominic Zaretti
- Dominic Zaretti – 38 yrs old, security expert, married to Sophie McIntyre

Supporting Characters

- Shane McIntyre – 37 yrs old, CEO and co-founder of McIntyre Security, Inc., Sophie's brother
- Beth McIntyre – 26 yrs old, Shane's wife
- Lia McIntyre – 25 yrs old, Jonah Locke's bodyguard and wife, Sophie's youngest sister
- Jonah Locke – 31 yrs old, rock star, married to Lia McIntyre
- Bridget McIntyre – 62 yrs old, Sophie's mother
- Calum McIntyre – 67 yrs old, Sophie's father
- Jamie McIntyre – 35 yrs old, Sophie's brother
- Molly Ferguson – 38 yrs old, Jamie's fiancée
- Jake McIntyre – 30 yrs old, Sophie's brother
- Annie McIntyre – 31 yrs, Jake's wife
- Hannah McIntyre – 28 yrs old, Sophie's sister
- Killian Devereaux – 35 yrs old, Hannah's boyfriend
- Owen Ramsey – 35 yrs old, Dominic and Sophie's friend

1

Sophie

Normally, I love parties, but not this evening. I'm due to deliver my first baby any day now, and I'm not at my best. I'm trying not to whine, but I feel like a beached whale and everything hurts. Dominic isn't helping. My husband has been hypervigilant for days now, ever since my doctor said, "Any day now, Sophie." He flinches every time I moan or wince. He hasn't taken his eyes off me since we arrived at my parents' house this evening for a family celebration.

I do my best to keep smiling, but the truth is I feel like crap. My back's been aching all day—all week, to be exact. And I've been having Braxton-Hicks contractions for the past several days. Dominic thinks I'm about to go into labor any second now. He's constantly hovering, never letting me out of his sight. You know... just in case.

Poor Dominic's a nervous wreck. He tries not to show it, but I can tell he's on edge about my impending delivery. The poor guy freaks out if I so much as get a paper cut, so the thought of me in labor is almost more than he can bear.

"Would you like some tea, sweetie?" Mom asks, as she hands me a comforting, warm cup. "It's your favorite—chamomile, decaf."

"Perfect." I close my eyes and take a sip. "Thanks, Mom. This is just what I needed." Mom always knows how to make things better. Luckily for me, I live next door to her and my dad. It's literally a 30-second walk from our house to theirs.

"How's Dominic holding up?" she asks as she glances across the room at my husband, who's currently hanging out with the guys at the bar. My dad's handing out beers and regaling them with stories about when he was a firefighter.

I can't hear what they're saying, but they sure are laughing a lot, and based on Dominic's expression, I suspect it's at his expense. They're probably giving him parenting advice, like tips on changing diapers.

I smile as I take another sip. "He's doing as well as can be expected. If I so much as flinch, he goes on red alert."

Mom smiles. "I remember those days. Calum was the same each time I was pregnant. After having so many kids, you'd think he would've gotten used to it eventually, but no." She pats my enormous baby bump. "Hang in there, sweetheart. It won't be long now."

The baby kicks, and I know Mom felt it because she grins at me. "I can't wait to hold my newest grandbaby."

"You and me both. I'll be so relieved when she's finally here."

I glance once more across the room at Dominic. My three eldest brothers are definitely giving him a hard time. My dad grins as he pats Dominic on the back.

We're here to celebrate the birthday of my youngest brother's new girlfriend, Jasmine. What a sweet girl. In spite of her awful upbringing and all the trauma she's suffered in her young life, she still manages to have a positive, upbeat attitude. I'm thrilled that my baby brother—Liam—has someone special in his life. He certainly deserves it.

The baby kicks me hard in the ribs, and I gasp. Dominic sets his beer bottle on the bar and heads toward me. "Everything okay, babe?" he asks as he joins me on the sofa. He lays his big hand on my thigh and squeezes gently.

I lay my hand on his. "I'm fine. She just kicked me in the ribs."

Dominic glances up at my mom. "How's she doing, really?"

Mom smiles. "She's holding up just fine, aren't you, sweetie?"

I nod. "Yep, that's me. I'm fine." *This baby can't come soon enough.*

The sound of laughter coming from the bar diverts our attention. My brother Jake approaches, a twin baby girl propped on each of his hips. He hands one of the babies to Dominic. "Here you go, buddy. You need as much practice as you can get."

"Gee, thanks," Dominic says as he grasps the little girl around her tiny waist.

I'm not sure which twin she is, but I think it's Emerly. It's hard to tell because they're identical. Only a few people can reliably tell them apart, namely their mother,

Annie; their big brother, Aiden; and my mom. Not even Jake gets them right one hundred percent of the time.

Jake deposits the second twin on Dominic's other thigh. Everly, I think.

Dominic does his best to wrangle the wriggling babies on his lap. "Funny, Jake. I only have two hands, you know."

Jake winks at me. "Just tryin' to be of help. The more practice he has, the better, right?"

"It's not like I've never held a baby before," Dominic says. "Sophie and I have done plenty of babysitting, you know. Your kids, plus Luke and Ava."

"Yeah, but Sophie probably does most of the childcare," Jake says. "Don't you, sis?"

Before I can respond, Dominic starts bouncing both babies gently. He's got a good hold on them, so I'm not too worried.

"Here, Uncle Dominic," six-year-old Aiden says as he approaches. He plucks the second baby off Dominic's lap and props her on his hip. "I'll help you. I'll hold Everly."

I was right!

The room fills with more laughter.

Jake reaches out and ruffles his stepson's spikey brown hair. "You're a good big brother, Aiden."

Before long, Emerly is snatched away by my youngest sister, Lia.

Dominic leans close and mutters, "They act like I don't know the first thing about babies."

Smiling, I reach up and stroke his bearded cheek. "You'll be a wonderful father, that much I know."

He snags my hand and brings it to his mouth to kiss. "Thanks, babe."

Half an hour later, after watching me wince a few times and listening to me blow out some heavy breaths, Dominic squeezes my hand. "It's time to head home."

I hate leaving the party when it's in full swing, but he's right. I need to go home and soak in a nice warm bath. Lately, it's one of the few things that truly relaxes me. "Sounds good to me. Let's go."

Dominic rises to his very considerable height, towering over everyone in the room—even my brothers, who are all over six feet tall. "Time for us to say goodnight," he says to the room at large. Then he reaches for my hands and helps me to my feet.

It takes a few minutes to say goodbye to everyone—there's lots of hugging and well wishes from my siblings, their spouses and significant others, and from the kids.

"Goodnight, Aunt Sophie," Aiden says as he gazes

up at me. Apparently, he traded his sister for Stevie, his stuffed Stegosaurus. "I hope your baby comes soon."

I reach out to ruffle Aiden's hair. "Thanks, kiddo."

"Goodnight, pal," Dominic says as he holds out his big fist. The two of them do a fist-bump.

After a few more hugs, Dominic walks me to the back door and out into the balmy spring night. We follow the smooth flagstone path that leads from Mom's house to ours.

When we step through the back door of our single-story house, Dominic sweeps me up into his arms and heads toward our bedroom. "I'll run your bath."

I lean my head against his broad shoulder as he carries me down the hallway. "My hero," I say with a sigh. "You know me so well."

"Sure I do," he says very matter-of-factly. "I'm your husband. It's my job to know you."

After Dominic deposits me on our big king-size bed, he disappears into the bathroom. I hear the water come on as he begins to fill the tub.

We have the most luxurious bathtub imaginable. Dominic is six-eight, and I'm six feet tall. We're not small people by any measure, and right now I'm as big as a house. I swear I count as a person-and-a-half. We have a large, round, sunken bathtub, easily big enough to seat four people. So, there's plenty of room for the two of us. I've been spending a lot of time in the tub, relaxing in warm water and letting the jet sprays massage my body. The tub does wonders for my aching back.

As I reach back to unzip my billowy maternity dress, I notice I have an audience.

Dominic is standing in the doorway to the bathroom, quietly observing me with an intensity that sends a shiver down my spine.

"Need some help with that?" he asks, his voice low and rough.

I smile. "Yes. As a matter of fact, I could use a little help." I turn my back in his direction, and a moment later I feel his warm fingers on the nape of my neck.

Cool air sweeps my newly exposed skin as he slowly lowers the zipper, but my chilled skin is soon warmed when his lips trail kisses across my shoulders and down my back. The dress slips off me and falls to the floor, leaving me in just my bra and panties.

Dominic's arms slide around me, resting beneath my heavy breasts. He kisses my neck, just behind my ear, and chuckles when I shiver. Then his hands slide up to cup my breasts, and he groans as he weighs them in his palms. "You're overdressed for bath time."

I unfasten the front closure of my bra, and the cups fall free, releasing my breasts into his hands. He squeezes the mounds gently, then brushes my sensitive nipples with the pads of his thumbs.

Now it's my turn to groan.

He grasps the waistband of my panties and slides them slowly down my legs. He kneels, and I brace one hand on his broad shoulder as I step out of my underwear. When I'm completely naked, he stands behind me once again and slides his hands around my torso, following the shape of my rounded abdomen.

Early in my pregnancy, when I first started to show, I was self-conscious about my body, but not anymore. Dominic has taught me to love the changes pregnancy has brought to my body—my bigger breasts, my firm rounded belly. Seeing how my body arouses him gives me a level of confidence I've never had before.

As one of his hands strokes my big belly, his other slides down between my legs to tease me. His fingers slide easily against my silky wet flesh. He teases me until I'm breathing hard and my knees feel weak.

"Ready for that bath?" he asks. And then he sweeps me into his arms and carries me into the bathroom.

The moment we step into the room, I'm hit with deliciously warm, humid air scented with lavender. Dominic read online that lavender is supposed to be relaxing, so he insists on adding lavender oil to my bath water.

He sets me on my feet beside the tub, then reaches down to test the temperature of the water. "It's perfect," he says.

He straightens, unbuttons his shirt, and tosses it aside. Then he steps close and presses his bare chest against mine. My highly-sensitized nipples tighten and tingle as they brush against the trim hair on his chest. I feel a corresponding tug between my legs, and suddenly more than my back is aching. My sex aches for him.

I read somewhere that pregnancy can heighten a woman's sex drive. For me, that's definitely true. My libido has been in high gear for the past few months. It seems like I'm always aching for him to fill me, and he's only too happy to oblige.

With one hand, he unfastens his jeans and lowers the zipper, while his other hand molds itself to one of my breasts, gently squeezing and shaping my flesh. He leans down and takes my nipple into his mouth, sucking gently, and a delicious shiver courses through me.

I cry out and press closer to him. He laughs as he

struggles to shove his jeans down with just one hand. Fortunately, he's already barefoot, so he doesn't have his boots and socks to contend with.

Finally, he manages to kick his jeans and underwear aside. He takes my hand and steadies me as I step into the tub.

"Oh, god," I moan as I carefully sink into the deliciously warm water. The water laps at my breasts.

Dominic steps in and lowers himself behind me. He leans back against the tub wall, parts his long legs, and pulls me between them, tucking me close against his groin. "Lean back," he says, his hands on my shoulders as he guides me back against him. "Better?"

"Mmm." I can't bring myself to speak coherently. This just feels too good.

He gathers my hair in his hands and twists the long strands into a top knot, which he secures with a handy scrunchy we keep in a bowl beside the tub.

"Scoot forward," he says, gently putting some space between us. He starts with my neck and shoulders, gently massaging my muscles. Gradually, he works his way down my back. I groan in pleasure, and he chuckles. When his hands reach my waist, he brings them back up to my shoulders and massages my arms down to my wrists. Then he takes one of my hands in his and massages my palm and fingers.

My head lulls back against his shoulder. "That feels so good."

He responds by trailing kisses down my neck to my shoulder. As he continues, I run my free hand up and down his thigh, squeezing and kneading the thick muscles.

I'm a big girl, but next to Dominic, I feel small and delicate.

As he sucks on the spot where my neck and shoulder meet, his hands return to my breasts. When a loud moan escapes me, he growls in response.

I feel a sudden kick right in the middle of my baby bump. "Whoa. That was a good one."

"Where?" Dominic presses a hand to my abdomen. "Show me."

I move his hand to the spot where I felt the baby kick, and we both wait with anticipation for a repeat. A moment later, she rewards us with a series of strong kicks in rapid succession. We both watch in fascination as my skin undulates.

After the baby settles down, Dominic slips a hand between my legs to gently tease my clit.

"Dominic." His name comes out as part-prayer and part-whimper.

"Yes? No?" he asks.

He's been so solicitous during my pregnancy, always asking, never taking anything for granted.

"Yes," I breathe. "Please, yes."

In a well-practiced move, Dominic climbs out of the tub and quickly dries himself off with a towel. Then it's my turn. After he helps me out of the water, he kneels before me holding a fresh towel and gently pats me dry.

He carries me into the bedroom and lays me down in the center of our big bed. I smile up at him as he climbs over me, on his hands and knees, caging me in.

The sight of his big body looming over me sparks a rush of desire and anticipation. He knows my body—every inch of it—and he knows how to make it sing.

He leans down and trails kisses from my cheek, down my throat, to the center of my chest.

Sighing, I relax and enjoy the pleasure. Dominic doesn't like to hurry. He takes his time, savoring every inch of my body, every touch, every taste. I settle back on the mattress knowing this is going to take a while.

As he works his way down my body, he pauses to kiss my abdomen. "Come on, peanut," he murmurs.

"Mommy and Daddy are waiting."

And then he skims his fingers over my abdomen and slips them between my thighs. His fingers are diabolical, as is his technique. Simultaneously, he teases my clit with this thumb while his long finger slides inside me and searches for my most sensitive spot. Once he finds it, he rubs tiny concentric circles, making me shake and shiver, not from the cool air on my hot, damp skin, but from the myriad of delicious sensations he's creating inside me. His thumb presses against my clit, massaging and teasing me until I'm squirming.

As a powerful orgasm rips through me, my legs stiffen, and my head bows back on the pillow. He continues stroking me through my climax, until my body slowly begins to relax, and I come down from the high.

He smiles as he comes up beside me and leans down for a kiss. "Doing okay, babe?"

"Mmm," I murmur. "Yes." I wrap my fingers around his thick erection and squeeze him firmly.

He groans low and rough. "Phee."

I love it when he uses his pet name for me.

Dominic rolls me over and lifts me up onto my hands and knees. Doggy style works best for us right now, with my abdomen being so big. I think he secretly prefers it because he likes to support my belly with one hand as he thrusts into me. Plus, he can sink *so deep* when he's kneeling behind me.

Slowly, carefully, he slides his enormous cock into me, all the way, until he's flush against my ass. He withdraws gently, then slips back in deep. Over and over, in a controlled rhythm, he pleasures us both while taking care not to knock me over.

The man's like a machine, able to go forever. If I were facing him, I know I'd see his jaw clenched tight, his teeth gritted, as he forced himself to hold on as long as he could.

I'm so aroused, I come again in a heated rush, pressing my hot face into the pillow to smother my cries.

"No," he growls as he gently turns my face. "I want to hear you. Let me hear you."

I smile as I whimper my way through another show of fireworks coursing through my body. It's one of the perks of pregnancy, at least for me. My body is so highly sensitized, my sex revved up and hungry for this man.

When my limbs melt, and I'm at risk of collapsing, Dominic allows himself to come. He sinks into me one last time, as deep as he can go. The force of his ejaculation, the heat and the rush, steals my breath.

The sound of his deep, guttural cry reverberates loudly in our bedroom.

After we've cleaned up in the bathroom, he tucks me into our bed and wraps me in his strong arms.

Dominic presses his lips to my forehead for the longest moment. "How do you feel?"

I smile. "Delicious."

"I didn't hurt you, did I?"

"No. You would never hurt me."

He tightens his hold. "I'd rather die first."

We lie together for a while, both of us settling down for the night, our pulses slowing, our breaths evening out.

"Rest up tomorrow," he says quietly as I'm about to doze off. "Nothing strenuous, okay? I want you to lie on the sofa, watch Netflix, and eat chocolate."

I chuckle. "I don't think eating a lot of chocolate is a good idea. I'm already as big as a house."

He runs his hand down my torso, tracing the round shape of my body. "You're a goddess." He leans close to kiss me. "I'm serious, though, about you taking it easy," he adds. "You're on maternity leave. No work, nothing strenuous. No lifting anything heavier than a dust bunny. If there's something that needs to be done, save it for me to do when I get home from work." He presses his lips to my shoulder. "Promise me, Phee."

"I promise."

2

Sophie

I'm barely conscious when Dominic silences his alarm the next morning. He's usually quick to rise from bed, but not today. He lingers, rolling close to me, spooning me, and burrowing his nose in my hair. His arm comes around me, tucked beneath my breasts, and he holds me close. "God, I wish I didn't have to go in this morning. I'd much rather stay home with you."

"Mmm," I murmur, only half awake. "Play hooky with me. I'll put in a good word with your boss." I chuckle. His boss is my brother Jake. After Dominic and I got married last fall, Jake offered him a job working with his surveillance team.

Dominic groans, then kisses my bare shoulder. "Jake asked me to attend a client meeting this morning. It shouldn't take more than a couple of hours. Once that's done, I'll head straight home. Remember, Phee, you promised. Sofa, Netflix, and chocolate. That's it. Nothing more."

I laugh. "I remember."

Then with a reluctant sigh, he forces himself to climb out of bed, grabs a change of clothes from our walk-in closet, and disappears into the bathroom to get ready.

"I'll be back as soon as I possibly can," he says when he returns from the bathroom and kneels on the bed, smelling faintly of cologne and mint toothpaste. He leans down to kiss me first, then my baby bump. "Don't you dare come before I get home, princess," he says to my belly. "Wait for Daddy." And then he kisses me one last time. "Love you."

"Love you," I murmur. As he leaves the room, I wrap my arms around his pillow, hug it close, and let sleep pull me back under.

* * *

The sound of my phone ringing wakes me up, and I check the time. It's eight-thirty. With a groan, I look at my phone screen and see that Alison is calling. Since I went on maternity leave, I left my very capable assistant in charge of my interior design business.

"Alison," I say, attempting to sound more awake than I am. "What's up?"

"Sophie, we have a problem," she blurts out. "I need you."

I sigh. "Alison, whatever it is, I'm sure you can handle it. If you need help, just ask Tristan."

"I can't. It's Gordon Cochran, again, and he says he'll speak only to you. I'm sorry, but that man is weird."

"He may be a bit weird, as you put it, but he's also one of our biggest clients. Did you get his new living room furniture installed yesterday?"

"Yes. And he says he hates it."

"What? Why? He approved all of the product photos and the design sketches."

"I know!" Alison says. "He's being completely unreasonable. I offered to make any changes he wanted, but he insists on talking to *you*. I told him you're on leave, but he didn't seem to care. He said if he doesn't see you, he's taking his business elsewhere."

I haul myself up into a sitting position and swing my feet to the floor. "All right. I'll go talk to him. I'm sure I can calm him down. God knows I've done it before."

"Thank you," Alison says. "I'm so sorry to bother you with this, but I didn't know what else to do. You know how he is."

"Yes, I know." Gordon Cochran is a glorified pain in the ass. He's also extremely wealthy and has very expensive taste. His penthouse apartment is located in one of the most prestigious residential buildings in Chicago. I don't want to lose him as a client. "Call him back, please, and tell him I'll be there in an hour."

I head to the bathroom to pee and wash up. There's no time for a shower. I remove the scrunchy still holding my hair in a top knot—a souvenir from last night—and painstakingly detangle my hair and brush it. Then I head for the closet to pull on one of my work-appropriate maternity tunics, super forgiving leggings, and a pair of extra-wide slip-on shoes. I swear my giant feet have swelled two sizes in pregnancy.

I make my way to the kitchen and make a quick scrambled egg, which I top with slices of avocado and shredded cheddar. I pair it with a buttered slice of whole grain toast and a cup of decaf coffee.

When the baby kicks, I press my hand to my abdomen. "*Decaf,*" I say to my offspring. "I hope you appreciate the sacrifices I'm making."

After I finish my breakfast, I rest a moment at the kitchen table because I've been up twenty minutes and already my back is hurting. I feel another one of those Braxton-Hicks contractions that have been plaguing me for the better part of a week.

"You need to come soon, sweetie pie," I say as I stroke my belly. "My back can take only so much. It's Daddy's turn to carry you around for a while." The mental image of Dominic carrying our baby around in one of those sacks strapped to his chest makes me smile.

The last thing I do before I leave the house is place a call to Dominic. He's going to be pissed that I'm going out to see an irate client, but it's better that I tell him up front than let him find out after the fact.

When my call goes straight to his voicemail, I realize he must be in his client meeting and his phone is on silent. I can override, but I don't want to interrupt his meeting when it's not anything terribly urgent. "Hi, honey. Um, I'm just calling to let you know that there's a problem with a client, and he's insisting that I come talk to him. I won't be gone long. I'm just driving to the client's apartment, have a quick discussion with him to soothe his ruffled feathers, and then I'll come straight home to do the sofa and Netflix thing. I promise. Please don't be upset. I'll be back home in under two hours tops, I promise. Love you."

And then I hang up, wincing as I envision Dominic's reaction when he gets my voicemail. Hopefully, he won't hear it until *after* his client meeting.

* * *

Gordon Cochran lives on the top floor of an exclusive high-rise apartment building in the Gold Coast—one of the most expensive real estate buildings in Chicago. As I pull into the parking lot of his complex, I park and head inside through the main entrance. With each step I take, I feel a sharp twinge in my abdomen. Those poor tendons are stretched to the limit. And my *back*—oh, my back. I'd give anything to sit in a warm bath right now. And one of Dominic's back rubs—I'd give anything for one of those, too.

The security guard nods when he sees me approaching the sign-in desk. "Good morning, Ms. McIntyre. You must be here to see Mr. Cochran."

Smiling, I nod as I sign in at the front desk. I've been called here so often over the past year that the security guards know me by name. I hope today's visit isn't going to be another wild goose chase. I swear, Gordon asks me to come over on the flimsiest of excuses. If I didn't know better, I'd think he was hitting on me. But he knows I'm married. I see my reflection in a mirrored wall across the lobby and almost chuckle at the sight of my enormous baby bump. Yes, I'm obviously taken.

I head for the bank of elevators and take the elevator up to the penthouse floor. From there, it's a short walk to his door. I knock, and the door opens almost immediately.

Gordon gives me a welcoming smile. "Sophie, come in, please." He opens the door wide and waves me inside. "You're looking particularly lovely today."

A shiver of unease crawls down my spine. The way he's looking at me is unsettling. Gordon Cochran is a giant mystery to me. He's clearly wealthy, but he never talks about what he does for a living. And whenever I ask what he does, he always gives me some vague answer about overseas commerce and global investment.

"How is everyone?" he asks. "How's your dear husband, Mr. Zaretti?" He motions to my belly. "And the little princess?"

"Fine. We're all fine." I feel a headache coming on, which is a perfect complement to my back ache. I just want to get this meeting over with so I can go back home.

Gordon might be eccentric, but he's been a good client. He likes to redecorate frequently, and he always pays his bills promptly. I really can't complain.

Today, he's dressed in a cream-colored linen suit with a sapphire blue silk hankie peeking out of his breast pocket. His thinning blond hair is slicked back. His complexion is a healthy shade of golden light brown thanks to his private suntanning booth. There's a diamond-encrusted Rolex on his left wrist, and a black diamond solitaire adorning the ring finger on his right hand. He looks as expensive as his taste in décor and art.

Alison said he was upset, but he doesn't seem so to me. In fact, he seems quite happy. "So, Alison tells me you're displeased with how your living room remodel turned out."

His smile widens. "Displeased? No. It's just that I prefer to deal directly with you, not with your assistant." His smile morphs into a frown. "I haven't seen much of you lately."

Out of habit, I lay my hand on my abdomen. "I've cut back on my hours until after the baby comes. I'm sure you can understand."

His smile returns. "Certainly. And now that you're here, I'd say everything is going to be just fine." He holds out his hand. "May I take your purse?"

Reluctantly, I hand it over, and he sets it on the console table next to the door.

"So, Gordon, what seems to be the problem? Alison said you wanted to see me about the final implementation of your new living room."

"Right! The living room. Come, let me show you."

I follow him across the foyer, through an arched doorway, into his formal living room. The new flooring, furniture, and wall treatment look exactly as they did in the design sketches he approved weeks ago. Standing in the middle of the room, I turn in a slow circle to take it all in. I can't find anything amiss. "So, what don't you like about the room?"

But he doesn't reply because he's too busy staring at my belly.

"Gordon?"

His gaze jumps to mine. "Sorry." He gestures to my

abdomen. "You've gotten so big since the last time I saw you. How soon are you due?"

"Any day now." I don't feel comfortable discussing my personal life with this man. "Now, about the living room?"

He continues to stare at me for the longest moment, an odd expression on his face, as if he's half intrigued and half disgusted by my condition. It's unsettling.

"How about some refreshments first?" he asks. "Can I get you something to drink? An iced tea, perhaps. Café au lait? Or how about some fresh-squeezed lemonade? My housekeeper made it just this morning."

I smile graciously, trying to ignore my physical discomfort. I really need to sit down. But better yet, I want to go home and get back in my big cozy bed. "Nothing for me, thank you."

He frowns. "Oh, come now, Sophie. Surely I can tempt you with something."

I have a feeling if I don't give in, we could be here all day. "Sure. Lemonade would be great, thank you."

"Coming right up. Why don't you have a seat and relax?" He motions to the pair of matching Queen Anne armchairs we installed as part of the remodel. "I won't be long."

I sit in one of the chairs and survey the room. I think it looks amazing. I can't imagine what he's going to complain about.

Wanting to check my phone to see if Dominic got my message yet, I reach for my purse before I remember Gordon took it from me and set it on the foyer table. Damn it. I hate being without my phone. I'm about to go retrieve it when Gordon walks back into the room carrying a silver serving tray holding two glasses of lemonade. He sets the tray down on a side table, picks up both glasses and hands me one. He takes a long sip from his glass. "Mm, delicious."

I take a sip of my drink—it is quite good, refreshingly cold with a perfect balance of sweetness and tart. I realize how thirsty I am and take a few more sips. Then I turn my attention back to the matter at hand. The sooner we get this over with, the sooner I can leave. "All right, so tell me, Gordon, what don't you like about this room? Whatever it is, I promise we'll fix it."

Gordon sets his glass down on the tray and watches me with a degree of scrutiny that's a bit unnerving.

As I'm watching him watch me, my vision starts to blur. I blink repeatedly but can't seem to focus.

"Sophie? Are you all right?"

Shaking my head, I try to set my glass down, but my hand shakes. Gordon takes the glass from me and sets it next to his. Suddenly, I feel dizzy, and the room starts to spin. "I don't feel so well."

"You do look rather flushed," he says.

"I really should get going. I'm supposed to be at home."

"You can't possibly leave in your condition." Gordon helps me to my feet and wraps his arm around my waist to steady me. "Come lie down until you feel better."

I shake my head, which makes the spinning worse. "No, I need to go home. Dominic's going to be so angry."

"No, he won't, love. Come with me. You'll feel better soon, I promise."

Before I realize it, I find myself walking into Gordon's bedroom. I put on the brakes. "No! I need to—"

He tugs me along with him. "What you need is to lie down, my love. You're not well."

I shudder when he calls me "*my love.*" It's creepy. The man needs to learn about personal space because he takes far too many liberties.

He walks me across the room, to the far wall, and stops. "What—"

"Steady there," he says when I waver on my feet. "We wouldn't want you falling. Not in your condition."

Suddenly, he lays his hand on the wall, and it slides open, leaving me staring into a dark cavern. When I open my mouth to speak, I realize my tongue and lips are numb.

Gordon's speaking, but I can't make out a word he's saying. My ears are ringing. He waves his hand in my face.

"Dominic." His name comes out as a garbled slur. "Where's Dominic?"

"Don't you worry about him. He's not here right now, but I am. I'll take very good care of you, I promise."

"No." The word comes out as an unintelligible slur. I shake my head. "Call Dominic."

"Sorry, my love, but that's not going to happen. Now come lie down before you fall down."

"Stop calling me that!" A few more steps, more stumbling. It's so dark in here I can't see where I'm going.

When my knees buckle, Gordon lowers me onto a soft, plush surface. "Don't worry, darling. I'll take good care of you."

Gordon switches on a brass lamp beside my head, and I realize I'm lying on a large, four-poster bed topped with a lacey white canopy.

I look up at Gordon. "Where am I?"

"Right where you should be." Then he looks off to his left and speaks to someone I can't see, someone lurking in the shadows beyond the bed. "Get her keys from her purse and take her Escalade. Dump it."

"Where, sir?" a male voice asks.

"Someplace where it won't be found any time soon. Take it to the South Side and leave it with the keys in it. I'm sure someone will help himself to it. The parts alone are worth a small fortune."

"Yes, sir."

"Then make sure all of the arrangements are finalized. We don't have much time."

My heart is pounding in my chest, so hard and so fast I can barely breathe. My brain is fuzzy, and I can't think straight. Gordon wraps something snugly around my wrist, and when I try to move my arm, I can't. "Let me up! What are you—what—"

And then, nothing. The lights go out.

3

Dominic

There are eight people seated at the long conference room table on the fifth floor of McIntyre Security. On one side of the table is Jake McIntyre, our team lead—who happens to be my brother-in-law—plus the rest of our team: Charlotte Mercer, Philip Underwood, and me. On the other side of the table is the executive management team from the Westdale Museum Center—the CEO, chief financial officer, VP of information technology, and one of their senior tech guys.

After experiencing a recent break-in that resulted in some very expensive and malicious vandalism, they're ready for a state-of-the-art security system—one that we can deliver. The CEO is clearly on-board with our plan for enhanced security at the museum center. Before, they opted for a lower ticket price. This time, they want the best security on the market, and that's ours.

At a quarter 'til noon, we adjourn the meeting, having come to an agreement. The only thing left is to sign the contract.

Everyone rises from the table. While Jake shakes the CEO's hand, I step out into the hall to check my messages. I have three voicemails and six text messages, but the only one I'm interested in is the one from Sophie. I bring up her voicemail message, smiling because I imagine she's going to ask me to bring her something home for lunch, like chicken tacos or a pizza. That woman's appetite lately has been impressive.

As I'm listening to her message, explaining to me why she needs to go visit a disgruntled client, I have to tamp down my irritation. I swear, I'm going to paddle her beautiful ass when I get home. She promised me she'd stay in and rest today. She's supposed to be on maternity leave. Hell, what do I have to do to get her to slow down? Tie her to the fucking bed?

I call her number, but it goes straight to voicemail. After the beep, I say, "Hey, babe, call me." I'm proud of myself for not sounding like an irate husband.

I wait a full minute before I try her again. Once more, my call goes straight to voicemail. *Fuck.*

So I pull up McIntyre Security's proprietary GPS tracking app on my phone to determine her current location. She'd better be home by now because it's almost noon.

The app comes back with an error message.

Location not found.

What the fuck?

I switch over to our home surveillance app to check our cameras to find the garage empty. Her Escalade's gone.

My heart starts hammering.

She's not at home.

So I go back to the GPS app and trace her movements from the moment she left home until she arrived at the client's home. Her last known location was at an apartment building in the Gold Coast, not far from the apartment building her brother Shane owns.

I call Alison, Sophie's assistant, a young twenty-something blonde fresh out of interior design school.

"McIntyre Interior Design," she says, answering the phone with an upbeat, professional tone. "Alison speaking."

"Alison, where's Sophie?"

"Oh, hey, Dominic. Um, where is she at this minute? I'm not sure. Isn't she at home?"

"No, she's not. Where did she go this morning?"

"To meet with a client."

"And what's the client's name?"

"Gordon Cochran."

"Address?" She rattles off an address on Lake Shore Drive. "And his phone number?" She gives me that as well. "If you hear from her, let me know ASAP." Then I hang up.

According to the tracking app, Sophie arrived at the client's building at nine-twenty-two a.m. The app shows her staying at that location until it loses her location thirty-six minutes later. There's no indication she ever left that building.

I pop my head back into the conference room and level my gaze on Sophie's brother. "Jake."

He stops mid-sentence in his conversation with the museum's CEO and looks at me with guarded intensity.

"What is it?"

"I have to go."

Jake's dark eyes narrow. "Everything okay?" He can tell from the tone of my voice that everything's *not* okay.

I give a curt shake of my head. "I need to check on someone." Some*one*, not some*thing*.

Jake nods just as curtly. *Message received.* "Call me if you need anything."

"Will do."

I race down the hallway toward the elevators, but there's a small crowd gathered outside the cars, waiting to get on. I don't bother hanging around, but instead, I make a sharp right turn and slam through the metal doors that lead to the stairwell. It's only five floors down to the parking garage. I'll get there faster on foot than I will waiting for a damn elevator.

I exit the stairwell in the underground parking garage and hop into my Yukon. As I start the engine and pull out of my parking spot, I call Sophie's mother. "Bridget, can you go check to see if Sophie's home? I don't think she is because her car's not there, but I need to know for sure."

Bridget sounds surprised. "Sure, I'll go right now. Is everything okay?"

I blow out a breath. "Honestly, I'm not sure. I just need you to confirm that she's not at home before I go off half-cocked."

"I'm already out the door," she says.

After ending the call, I pull out of the garage, turning left on N. Michigan Avenue, and head west toward Lake Shore Drive. It's a quick fifteen-minute drive to the client's apartment building. I park in the front and get out of my SUV to do a quick visual scan of the parking lot, but there's no sign of Sophie's gray Escalade.

Bridget calls me back as I'm heading inside the building. "She's not at home. I checked the whole house. Dominic, what's going on? Where is she? Is something wrong?"

"I'm working on it, Bridget. I'll let you know as soon as I find her." And then I hang up.

I push through the front glass doors and into an upscale lobby with white marble floors, marble columns, lots of potted trees and exotic flowers, and a three-tiered water fountain.

A uniformed security guard stationed in the lobby halts my progress toward the elevators. "Can I help you, sir?"

"I need to get upstairs, to the penthouse."

He purses his lips. "Name, please?"

I frown, giving him a look that cowers most men. "Why?"

The guy winces. "I'm sorry, sir, but I need to check the guest list to make sure you're on it."

I'm sure as hell not on any fucking guest list. "McIntyre," I say, when inspiration hits. "I'm from McIntyre Interior Design. Sophie McIntyre asked me to come. We're meeting with a client upstairs. Gordon Cochran."

The guard consults an app on his phone. "Yes, it's right here—McIntyre." Looking more than a little relived, he nods as he motions me through the turnstile. "Go right on up, sir. Top floor, apartment four."

I stalk toward the elevator and grab an empty one, taking it to the top floor. When I exit the car, I'm in a hallway. There are four apartments on the top floor. I head for the one I want.

My heart is threatening to bust out of my chest as I knock on the door. When there's no answer, I knock again, louder this time. It takes every bit of self-restraint I have not to kick open this fucking door. According to the tracking app, my wife's inside.

Just as I'm about to pound the door with my fist, it opens. A slender blond middle-aged man with pale blue eyes glances up at me. He's dressed in an expensive, light-colored suit that probably costs more than I make in a month. "Can I help you?" he says.

"Are you Gordon Cochran?"

He nods. "Yes."

I shove my way inside, and Cochran jumps back to keep from being plowed under. "Where is she?"

"Where's who?" The man scowls, as if he has no idea what I'm talking about.

"Sophie?" I glance around a sparsely furnished foyer, looking for any sign of my wife, but there's nothing here but a table holding a vase of expensive-looking flowers.

I cross the foyer and walk through an arched doorway that leads into what must be the living room. "Sophie!"

Cochran follows me, shaking his head in confusion. "You can't just barge into my home, sir. Don't make me call the police."

I round on him and level him with a glare. "Where is she, Cochran?"

"Sophie was here, yes," he says in a smooth voice. "We had a meeting at nine-thirty, we spoke for about thirty minutes, and then she left. I'm afraid I don't know where she is now."

He's lying. According to my app, she arrived, but never

departed. "Then you won't mind if I have a look around, will you?"

He frowns, and I'm sure he's going to say no. But then his composure returns, and he nods. "I don't mind. Anything for Sophie."

For a moment, my gaze locks onto Cochran's. I don't like the man. I especially don't like that he was perhaps the last person to see Sophie.

The apartment is huge, so it takes me a while to search the entire place. I move systematically from room to room, checking every closet, every cupboard. I search every bedroom, bathroom, the kitchen, pantry, home gym, theater room, utility room. I look *everywhere*, and I find absolutely nothing. There's no sign that she was ever here.

After I've made a full circuit of the place, I end up back in the foyer.

"As I said, she left about an hour ago." Cochran sounds way too satisfied, almost relieved. "I'm sorry I can't be of more help."

He's lying.

"Thank you, Mr. Cochran," I say, managing to keep my voice civil. "I appreciate you humoring me."

"Of course," the man says. Relief spreads across his

face, and he smiles. "Anytime."

Even though it kills me to go, I exit the apartment and head back down to the lobby. I need more information before I can determine my next steps. I stop at the guard's desk. "Where's your security office?"

The young man points at a door across the lobby marked PRIVATE.

I knock on the door, and it promptly opens.

An older African-American man wearing a black security uniform looks me in the eye. According to his name tag, his name is Al Montgomery. "Can I help you?" he asks.

I grab my wallet and flash him my McIntyre Security ID. "I need to see your CCV footage from the front parking lot, from approximately nine a.m. until noon."

The man frowns. "You're not a cop. I don't have to show you anything."

I dig in my wallet and pull out a photo of Sophie, practically shoving it in the man's face. "This is my *wife*. My very *pregnant* wife. She arrived here at approximately nine-thirty a.m., and now she's missing."

Montgomery stares closely at the photo of Sophie. "I remember seeing her come into the lobby." He nods as he motions me toward a desk holding a number of computer monitors. "I'll show you what you want to see," the man says as he sits in a chair and slides up to the desk.

I stand behind him, looming over his shoulder as I watch him as he starts scrubbing through the past couple hours of video footage.

"That's her," I say, pointing at the monitor as a gray Escalade pulls into the parking lot. I watch the footage as she parks, gets out of the SUV, and walks into the building. "Speed forward about thirty minutes." I watch as the video plays in fast forward until I see the Escalade pull out of the parking lot. "That's my wife's vehicle. Back it up. I want to see who's driving it."

Montgomery does as I asked, rewinding the video until we spot someone—a man with black hair and a trim beard, dressed in black—get in her car. I lean closer to study the footage. "Do you recognize him?"

Montgomery nods. "Yeah. That's Mr. Cochran's assistant, Mr. Lane."

We let the footage run again and watch as Lane gets into the Escalade and pulls out of the parking lot, turning right onto Lake Shore Drive.

"Thanks," I say to Montgomery. I grab my phone and call Jake. "We have a problem."

"What?"

"I can't find Sophie." I give him a rundown of what I know, what the GPS app shows, and where she was last seen. Then I give him Cochran's address.

"We're on our way," Jake says. "Don't worry. We'll find her."

We. He's bringing the whole team—Charlie and Philip, too.

4

Sophie

Slowly, my brain comes back online and I wake from a deep sleep. My head is pounding, and I hurt all over. My eyes don't seem to be working right. I blink several times, trying to clear my vision, but I still can't see anything. It takes me a moment to realize I can't see because I'm in total darkness. There's no window in this room, no light, nothing.

I remember I'm lying on a bed, a big four-poster bed with a white canopy overtop. When I try to move my arms, searing pain shoots to my shoulders to my skull, and I cry out. It takes me a second to realize I can't move my arms at all—my wrists are secured to the headboard. I pull against the restraints, but that only hurts more. My ankles are secured to the footboard.

I fight anyway, hoping I can free myself, but it doesn't help.

The door opens, and light from another room streams inside.

"Please don't struggle, my love," Gordon says as he walks into the room. "You'll only hurt yourself, and we don't want that, do we?"

Gordon takes a seat in an armchair beside the bed. He crosses one leg over the other and leans back casually. His hands are clasped in his lap, and he looks like he hasn't a care in the world. He smiles. "Head clearing up now? I fear I might have given you a bit too much."

"Too much of what?"

"A sedative."

"You gave me a sedative!" I screech at him, furious that he might have hurt my baby.

"I would have given you more if I could have, but I didn't want to risk the health of the baby. But don't you worry! She's perfectly safe. I did my research beforehand."

"Are you insane?"

"No. I'm a man used to getting what he wants. As for the sedative—" he smiles like he's proud of himself "—I slipped it into your lemonade. It's completely tasteless. You never suspected a thing, did you?"

I tug once more on my restraints—which now I can see are black leather cuffs—but they don't give an inch. I still for a moment and take a deep breath as I try to get myself under control. This is not the time to panic. "Gordon, you need to let me go." I use my calm, assertive voice.

He winces. "I'm afraid it's too late for that. I've already played my hand."

I glance around the dimly-lit, windowless bedroom. "Where am I? What is this place?"

"It's a secret chamber within my bedroom. Clever, isn't it?"

The gloating in his tone makes me lose it, and I start struggling again, this time trying to free my ankles, but they too are secured by leather cuffs. My god, this place is like a BDSM dungeon. "Let me go, Gordon!" I growl low in my throat. I'm losing patience with this imbecile. "Right this minute. I'm warning you—"

He smiles apologetically. "You're beautiful when

you're angry, did you know that?"

My stomach turns, and a sour taste shoots up into my mouth. "You are insane."

"Hardly. I'm just a man who knows what he wants."

My brain still feels foggy, and I'm having trouble putting all this together. I realize I have more important things to worry about when a sharp pain ripples across my abdomen, leaving me gasping. "Gordon, seriously, you have to let me go. I'm pregnant."

He chuckles. "Yes, I had noticed. It's unfortunate, but I can make it work."

"Make what work?"

"*Us.* You and me. And now baby makes three. But don't worry, I'm fine with the baby. We're all going to be very happy."

I stare up at the canopy and grit my teeth in frustration. "My husband's going to kill you."

He smirks. "Don't be so sure, dear. That Neanderthal has already been here and gone. Undoubtedly, he's running around town on a wild goose chase searching for your vehicle, which is long gone and probably being stripped for parts as I speak."

"You can't do this, Gordon. You have to let me go." I take a deep breath and force myself to calm down. "Just let me go, and we'll pretend this never happened, okay?" I'm lying through my teeth, but he doesn't have to know that.

He chuckles. "Sorry, darling. It's not going to happen." He stands and checks his Rolex. "Ready for lunch? There's a spinach quiche waiting for us."

He nods across the room at an open door. "Do you need to visit the little girls' room? You have your own private facilities at your disposal. In fact, you have all you could possibly need. I thought of everything and spared no expense. And, in case you're worrying about the baby, I have a midwife on standby."

When Gordon's phone chimes, he glances at the screen. "That was fast," he mutters. "But not unexpected. I won't be long, dear." He opens the top drawer of the bedside table and withdraws a ball gag.

"You wouldn't dare," I say in a low voice as I stare at the device.

He forces the rubber ball into my mouth and secures the Velcro straps securely behind my head.

I try to speak but can't utter a single intelligible word. He's trying to keep me quiet so no one can hear me scream for help.

My stomach sinks like a stone. Even if someone comes

looking for me, they'll never find me in his hidden chamber. No one would think to look behind a wall.

"Sorry about the gag, my love. I know it's a cliché, but it's only temporary—just until I get rid of our unwanted guest."

Dominic.

It has to be. My dread turns quickly to desperate optimism. *He's here.*

There are two things I am absolutely sure of.

First, Gordon Cochran is insane.

And second, my husband is going to tear this penthouse apart looking for me.

Gordon slides open a panel in the wall, steps through it, then slides it back into place.

"Dominic!" I scream. Or, at least I try to scream. Because of the gag, I can't make much of a sound. Certainly not enough that anyone on the other side of that wall can hear me.

I try to remain calm, breathing steadily through my nose, as I listen intently for sounds of rescue. A few minutes gradually turn into a lot of minutes, and still that wall panel remains in place.

Another searing pain travels across my abdomen, stealing my breath, and I suck in air through my nose.

That wasn't a Braxton-Hicks contraction.

That was the real thing.

Pressure in my abdomen starts to build, and soon I feel like something heavy is sitting on me, crushing my diaphragm, and making it hard to breathe.

Please hang in there, baby girl. Now's not the time to make an appearance.

5

Dominic

This time, when I pound on the door to penthouse apartment four, it opens promptly. There stands Gordon Cochran with a self-satisfied smile on his smarmy face. "Mr. Zaretti, you're back."

I push past the door, grab Mr. Smarmy by his shirt collar, and slam him against the wall. *"Where's my fucking wife?"*

His pale blue eyes widen. "I don't know what you're talking about. I told you, she left a long time ago. I hope you don't expect me to keep track of her for you."

I twist my grip on his collar, cutting off his air. He doesn't panic, though. He eyes me steadily, like a man who thinks he has the upper hand. "Where is she?" I demand through gritted teeth. "I know she's here."

"Her car—is gone. Check—the parking—lot." He barely manages to eek out those few words as he struggles to catch his breath.

I shake my head. "I'm not an idiot, Cochran. I saw the building's surveillance footage. It wasn't Sophie who drove off in her SUV. It was your assistant."

I see a flash of indecision in the man's eyes, but he recovers quickly. He coughs. "Can't—breathe. Killing me—won't help—you—find her."

I loosen my hold, but keep him pinned to the wall like the bug he is. "Where is she?"

When I shake him, he gasps, "I have—no idea."

"You're lying." When I release him with a shove, he stumbles as he sucks in air, his hand going to his throat as he feels for injuries. "Then you won't mind if I search the place again."

"I'm afraid you're wasting your time, Mr. Zaretti. You've already searched my home and found nothing. I promise, you won't find her here."

Without bothering to wait for the others to arrive, I start searching the apartment again, retracing my steps from earlier, but going more slowly this time. She's here somewhere. I know it in my gut. I just have to find her. This place is huge, which means there's plenty of space to hide a person.

With Cochran dogging my every step, I pass through a side door that leads from the foyer to the kitchen, where I find a silver serving tray on the counter. There are two glasses—one empty and the other one about a third full. I pick up the partially full glass and smell the contents. *Lemonade.* There's a smudge of pink lipstick on the rim. It's Sophie's favorite shade of lipstick.

Bingo.

She was here, and she drank some of this lemonade. I smell the liquid again, hoping to catch a trace of a substance that shouldn't be in there, but I can't detect anything. That doesn't mean he didn't drug her. I figure he must have slipped something into her drink because Sophie's not a pushover. Cochran is tall, yet slender. He'd have a hard time overpowering Sophie, even in her current condition. She probably outweighs him by close to forty pounds. She's not shy. She would have fought back... unless she was incapacitated. *Drugged.*

My stomach knots at the idea of Sophie being drugged. I just hope whatever he used isn't something that could hurt the baby.

I turn to loom over him. "What'd you give her?"

"I have no idea what you're talking about." His expression tightens, just enough to give him away. He's worried.

A moment later, I hear Jake's booming voice coming from the foyer. "Dominic!"

"In the kitchen!"

A moment later, Jake joins us, followed by Philip and Charlie.

Jake looks fit to be tied. He's a big guy—like me. He's dark and intense and right now he looks like he's ready to bash in some heads. I know the feeling.

I nod to the glass of lemonade. "That's evidence. Somebody keep that safe. The rest of you, help me search the apartment. Check *everywhere*."

"I've had enough!" Cochran says. "You can't just barge into my home like this. This is private property. I'm calling the police."

"Go right ahead," I say. "You'll be saving us time."

Jake, Philip, and I fan out to search, while Charlie stays behind to guard the evidence. Cochran follows behind me.

I check the kitchen, the butler's pantry, storage closets, bedrooms, the staff quarters. I make my way through the apartment, examining every inch, all the while yelling Sophie's name at the top of my lungs. Occasionally I pause to listen for the slightest tell-tale sound.

Nothing.

Gut instinct has me returning once again to Cochran's bedroom, which I've already searched twice. I scan the room thoroughly, looking for a sign—any sign—of Sophie's presence.

Cochran watches me from the doorway, his arms crossed indignantly over his chest. "Get out of my room."

Ignoring him, I walk the perimeter of the room, examining built-in bookcases, a large flatscreen TV mounted on the wall, a gas fireplace, a reading nook with two chairs and a wooden table between them. On the table is a crystal vase filled with long-stemmed red roses.

I happen to glance down at the floor, at the leg of one of the chairs, and I notice that the chair was recently moved. I can tell because one of the chair's feet isn't sitting in the impression in the carpet.

Somebody moved that chair.

My gaze goes to the wall behind the chair. The room

is expensive, like the rest of this place. The walls are decorated with floral wallpaper.

I study the wall, pounding my knuckles across the surface and noting the dull thud of the solid wood framing behind it. I move along the entire wall, knocking every few inches until I hit paydirt. The sound here is different—it's hollow.

Cochran steps away from the door, coming further into the room. "It's time for you to leave, Mr. Zaretti." His voice has changed, dropped an octave. His facial features tighten before my eyes. "This violation of my privacy has gone on long enough." He whips his phone out of his pocket. "I'm calling the police."

"Yeah, you do that," I tell him as I run my hands up and down the wall, searching for a mechanism to open it. Finally, I press my palms against the wall and attempt to slide it. With enough pressure, the wall panel starts to give way, and I glimpse a dark, cavernous space behind it.

Son of a bitch! "Jake! Here!"

Cochran grabs my arm and attempts to pull me back. "I said get out of my house!"

I shake him off and pull a penlight from my jacket pocket, flick the switch, and shine the light into the dark cavity of the room before me. I spot furniture—a chair, a dresser, the foot of a four-poster bed.

Cochran grabs my arm and attempts to haul me back. "Sophie!" I yell.

Philip arrives just in time to grab Cochran and pulls him off me.

"Don't let him go," I tell Philip, who has Cochran's wrists pinned behind his back.

I reach into the room behind the wall and locate a light switch just inside the opening and flip it, turning on an overhead chandelier. My heart slams against my ribs as I race inside. "Sophie!"

I head straight to the ornate bed and pull the canopy aside. There she is, secured to the bedframe with black leather cuffs on her wrists and ankles. Her face is streaked with tears, her mascara running. She seems half-blinded by the overhead light. My heart nearly stops and my blood burns when I see the ball gag in her mouth. I'm going to kill that son-of-a-bitch.

Her eyes are open wide, her expression panicked as she struggles against her restraints.

"Sophie, I'm here," I say as I approach the bed slowly, not wanting to frighten her. "It's all right."

The moment she recognizes my voice, she slumps

against the mattress.

My vision turns red, and I want so badly to turn around and choke the life out of Cochran, but there's no time for that. "She's here!" I yell to Philip.

I reach down to unfasten the ball gag and gently pry it out of Sophie's mouth.

"Dominic!" Her face twists, and she cries out in pain as her entire body is seized in a powerful grip.

That's when I notice the bedding beneath her hips is wet. Her water must have broken.

Quickly, I unfasten her wrist and ankle restraints, then help her into a sitting position.

Eyes wide, she clutches my shirt. "The baby—I'm in labor."

"Everything's going to be fine. I'll get you to the hospital." I scoop her into my arms and carry her out of the room. I lean over and kiss her damp forehead. "I've got you, babe."

Jake rushes into the room and comes to an abrupt stop, seeing that I've got her. His expression darkens when he gets a good look at his sister.

"Call the police," I say as I head for the door.

Jake follows me out into the hallway. "Do you want me to call an ambulance?"

"No. I can get her to the hospital faster on my own." I nod back toward Cochran, who's being restrained by Philip. Then I look to Jake. "I want him arrested for kidnapping, and that's just for starters. Then call your folks and tell them to meet us at the hospital. Call Shane, too. And the attorney. Call everyone."

I carry my wife out of the building and sit her gently in the front passenger seat of my vehicle. She's shaking as I buckle her seat belt. "It's going to be okay," I tell her in a calm, steady voice. I'm not calm at all, but that's what she needs to hear from me. I lean in and kiss her cheek.

She tenses in her seat, shuts her eyes, and starts panting. "Contraction." One word—that's all she manages to say before her face screws up in pain.

A second later, I'm in the driver's seat and we're on our way to the hospital.

6

Sophie

I have a death grip on the door handle of the Yukon, and my other hand is clutching my seatbelt for dear life. Dominic's speeding through traffic as fast as he dares without risking an accident. It'll be a miracle if we aren't pulled over by the police. All I can do is concentrate on breathing and grit my teeth as I endure the excruciating pressure on my torso.

Dominic lays his hand on my thigh. "Hang on, babe. We'll be there soon."

Hang on. That's easier said than done. "Dominic, I'm worried. Gordon drugged me with something, some kind of sedative. I'm worried that it might have hurt the baby. He said it wouldn't, but I don't believe a word he says."

His hand moves from my thigh to my abdomen. "Do you feel her moving?"

"Yes." I gasp when a powerful contraction squeezes my midsection, cutting off my breath. Dominic's hand on my belly tightens as he makes a sharp right turn. We're almost there. I can see the hospital up ahead.

Dominic turns into the ER parking lot and pulls right up to the double glass doors marked ENTRANCE. Leaving the vehicle running, he jumps out the driver's door and comes around to my side. My door flies open, and he reaches in to unbuckle my seat belt and scoop me into his arms.

"We need some help here," he shouts as he rushes me through the double doors. "My wife's in labor."

A young woman in a hospital uniform rushes up with a wheelchair. "Here, sir. Sit her down here."

When Dominic lowers me onto the wheelchair, I double over in pain and wrap my arms around my abdomen.

"I'll take her back," the young woman says. Then she

nods across the crowded waiting room. "Can you go to the information desk and sign her in?"

"I'm not leaving her," Dominic says as he sticks by my side.

"Please, sir, you need to sign her in."

"It's all right. I'll do it," says a familiar voice from behind us.

I glance back to see my mom standing there, my dad beside her. They both look stressed. Dad's arm is around my mom's shoulders.

Mom's here. Thank god.

"Thanks, Bridget," Dominic says, and then he follows me through the door to the treatment area.

"Honey, I'll be with you as soon as I can!" Mom calls as the door closes behind us.

"Dominic." My voice is shaking.

He reaches for my hand. "I'm right here, babe. Everything's going to be fine, I promise."

"Don't leave me, Dominic, please."

"Never." His voice sounds rough, and I suspect he's just as scared as I am.

After that, everything happens in a flash. An ER doctor assesses my vitals before I'm wheeled to the maternity ward and transferred to a bed in a private room. A nurse comes in to help me get out of my clothes and into a hospital gown.

Another nurse hurries into my room. "Hello, Sophie. I'm Claire, your labor and delivery nurse. I'll be assisting Dr. Goddard today."

Dominic tells her about the sedative I was given and immediately she checks my vitals, and then the baby's heart rate.

"Everything seems okay, but I'll make sure Dr. Goddard knows. She'll probably want to do some bloodwork." She checks over my records and hooks me up to some monitors. "We'll be keeping an eye on your heart rate and blood pressure, as well as the baby's heart rate. Let's find out just how far along you are, okay?"

As she eases me into position, she glances up at Dominic. "Would you like to wait out in the hallway while I'll check your wife?"

Without saying a word, he crosses his arms over his chest, not budging an inch.

I chuckle. "He's staying."

The nurse smiles, too. "I can see that. Okay. I'm just going to check your cervix."

The nurse gently reaches between my legs. "Seven centimeters. I'll call Dr. Goddard." She gives me a smile.

"It won't be long now."

"Can someone please find Sophie's mother?" Dominic asks the nurse. "Bridget McIntyre. She was downstairs in the ER, checking Sophie in."

Claire nods. "Yes, don't worry. We'll send someone to find her."

Another contraction starts ramping up, and I lie back in bed and reach for Dominic's hand.

"Can you give my wife something for the pain?" he asks. "When does she get the epidural?"

Claire heads for the door. "We'll clear that with her doctor, of course, but it should be very soon. We'll get someone in here as quickly as possible."

Dominic sits on the side of my bed and takes both of my hands in his.

There's a knock on the door, and then my brother Shane pops his head in the door. "The police are here, wanting to get a statement from Sophie."

"Not right now," Dominic says, his voice loud enough that anyone in the hallway would be able to hear him. "Tell them she's busy having a baby. Tell them Gordon Cochran drugged her and restrained her to a bed. He fucking kidnapped her. What else do they need to know?"

Shane grins. "I've already told them they'll have to wait to talk to her. By the way, Cochran was picked up by the police and is currently being held in the county jail, charges pending."

"The man's insane," Dominic says to Shane. "As soon as I get a chance, I'm going to fucking kill him."

A laugh bursts out of me, followed by a grimace. "Not funny right now."

Dominic looks my way. "I wasn't trying to be funny."

"Let's hold off on the killing part and let the cops do their thing," Shane says. "They're working on locating Sophie's SUV and Cochran's accomplice." Shane looks away down the hall, then back at us. "And here comes Mom."

A second later, Mom walks into the room. Her eyes are red, as if she's been crying.

"I'm all right, Mom," I tell her, hoping to calm her nerves.

Mom looks to Dominic. "Is she?"

He scowls, but nonetheless says, "I guess. She's having a baby."

Mom comes around to the other side of my bed and reaches for my hand, cradling it in hers. "I didn't know what to think when Jake called. He said someone was keeping her hostage at his home. What does that mean? How is that even possible?"

Another contraction starts, and I grit my teeth. "Here it comes."

Dominic squeezes my hand. "Maybe we should talk about this later," he says to Mom, his worried gaze on me.

Mom brushes my hair back from my hot, damp face. "It's okay, honey. Just breathe through it." And then she demonstrates.

Before long, a man comes into my room to administer the epidural. "I just spoke to Dr. Goddard, and she okayed the epidural."

Mom and Dominic stand back to give the man room to work. Once the line is in, I'm allowed to settle back on the bed.

Mom pulls a chair to the side of my bed and sits. "It's going to be fine," she says, squeezing my hand as she gives her signature mom smile—the one that says "everything's going to be all right."

I need that kind of encouragement right now. I'm scared. I'm not afraid to admit it. I'm worried about our baby. I just want to know that she's okay.

Dominic pulls a chair up to the left side of the bed and

reaches for my free hand, cradling it securely in his. If I'm scared, Dominic is terrified, although he does a good job of hiding it. He has a hard time coping with the thought of me being in pain.

Mom glances past me and studies Dominic's stoic expression. "Relax, honey," she tells him. "She's doing fine."

He nods but doesn't say anything. He just tightens his grip on my hand.

I nod, but before I can speak, I feel that tell-tale tightening around my middle. "Another contraction," I say, pressing my head into my pillow. The head of the bed is propped up at a comfortable angle.

"Try to relax and breathe through it," Mom says. Her voice is low and soothing, and it helps ground me.

At the height of the contraction, I hold my breath, squeeze my eyes shut, and grit my teeth. For my husband's sake, I'm trying not to be dramatic about it.

When I feel his heavy palm on the top of my head, I smile.

As the epidural has more time to work its magic, the contractions start to feel less intense. Between the waves, I try to relax, close my eyes, and conserve my energy. There's no telling how long this will go on.

Mom and Dominic chat quietly, their voices floating

above me, and it's comforting. Dad pops his head in occasionally to check on me. Over the next hour, I hear my brother Shane's voice coming from somewhere outside my room, along with Jake's voice and Jamie's and Liam's.

"All the kids are here," Mom tells me. "They're gathering in the waiting room down the hall. The girls are here, too—Lia, Beth, Molly, Annie."

During one of my rest breaks, my mind drifts back to the time last fall when Dominic saw me in the courtroom when I testified against his half-brother, Mikey Alessio, for the cold-blooded murder of assistant district attorney Kent Martinez—my blind date that evening. I'd come back to Chicago after Dominic left me at the cabin in Tennessee to join Franco Alessio's—his father's—criminal syndicate. Dominic sacrificed his own freedom in order to protect me—in exchange for his father canceling the hit on me.

I can still picture the look on Dominic's face when I walked past him in the courtroom and he saw how sick I looked. He thought I was ill. He didn't know I was pregnant. It wasn't until he came after me that he discovered I was carrying his child. Fortunately for us, Franco loved Dominic enough to let him out of his agreement, paving the way for us to be together.

That day in the courtroom was the only time I'd seen Dominic cry, until today. When he found me in that awful hidden room at Gordon's, there were tears in his eyes, and they tracked down his cheeks as he removed the restraints holding me to that bed.

But right now, at my bedside in the maternity ward, his eyes are clear and filled with determination as if to say, *"We'll get through this."*

Claire returns a while later to check me and announces that I'm dilated to ten centimeters. "I'll go get your doctor."

What follows is a whirlwind of activity as our beautiful baby girl comes into the world. It's all a blur to me. I just remember my doctor instructing me to push, push, push, while Claire encouraged me with a kind voice. Mom and Dominic each held one of my hands through it all.

A little while after our daughter is born, Dr. Goddard invites Dominic to cut the cord. I see tears in his eyes again, only this time they're tears of joy. "Babe, she's beautiful," he says.

Claire lays our daughter on my bare chest, her little cheek resting against my breast. "Hello there, little angel," I whisper. "Welcome to the world."

* * *

Two days later, Mia Olivia Zaretti and I are discharged from the hospital. After double-checking and triple-checking that the infant car seat is installed correctly in the back seat of his Yukon, Dominic drives us home. I've never seen him drive so cautiously before, but I bite my lip and refrain from teasing him. He's still adjusting to the idea that he's a father now.

When we pull up into our drive, the first thing I see is my lovely Escalade parked in front of the garage. Apparently, the police located it in the South Side of Chicago, and after they finished searching it for evidence, Jake sent Philip to retrieve it and bring it here.

It looks like most of the lights are on inside the house. Mom said she and Dad would be there making sure everything was set up for the baby's arrival.

The nursery is already put together—the crib, the changing table, the little white dresser with a mirror hanging above it, the padded rocking chair. Mia's sleepers are neatly folded and tucked into the dresser drawers. Tiny dresses hang in the nursery closet. The white wicker basket on the floor is filled with the softest stuffed animals imaginable. The bookcase shelves are lined with board books for infants.

My parents greet us at the door as we come in through the garage.

I step inside first, into the kitchen. Dominic comes in right behind me carrying Mia in her car seat.

My mom is practically buzzing with excitement as she peers down at her newest granddaughter, who is sound asleep. "Can I hold her?"

"She slept the entire way home," Dominic says proudly as he sets the car seat on the kitchen table. He steps aside as Mom moves in.

"The others wanted to be here, too," she says as she carefully unbuckles Mia, "to greet you and welcome little Mia home, but I suggested they wait until tomorrow and let you settle in first." She lifts Mia out of the car seat and cradles her to her chest. "Oh, Calum, just look at her."

Dad peers over Mom's shoulder. "She looks just like Sophie did when she was born."

"I think so, too." Mom gently strokes Mia's wispy brown hair.

Dominic goes back into the garage, then returns a few minutes later carrying my overnight bag and Mia's. "She's beautiful, just like her mama," he says as he leans in to kiss my cheek. He meets my gaze. "You need to either sit on the sofa or go lie down in bed. Which will it be?"

"The sofa," I say, pointing to the family room just off the kitchen. "I've been in bed for most of the past two days. I'd like to stay up for a bit."

Dominic takes my hand and leads me to the sofa, where I settle myself very gingerly on the seat cushion. Things are very sore down there.

Mom brings Mia and comes to sit beside me.

When Dominic's phone rings, he checks the screen, scowls, and then steps into the other room to take the call.

"I wish Dominic's mother could be here, too," I say as I gaze down at my sleeping daughter. I might be a bit biased, but I think she's the most beautiful baby I've ever seen.

Mom glances down at Mia. "I think it's wonderful that you named her after Dominic's mother. She'd be very touched."

Dominic doesn't talk about it much, but I know he misses his mother terribly. His relationship with his father is strained at best. His maternal grandparents, who raised him, have passed, and he doesn't have any family other than his father. But he has me, and now our daughter. And my family has welcomed him with open arms.

When Dominic rejoins us, he sits on my other side. "That was Franco. He called to congratulate us on the birth of our daughter." He scowls. "He wants to see her."

I'm not sure how I feel about having a mob boss in our home. "What did you say?"

"I told him we'd discuss it and get back with him."

"And how did he react?"

Dominic shrugs. "He seemed pretty calm about it. I think he's being on his best behavior because he really wants to see his granddaughter."

"Of course he does. She's his granddaughter."

"I just don't want any part of his life touching ours, certainly not our daughter's life."

"Don't you think it might cause more problems if we *don't* let him see her? He's kept his word where I'm concerned."

Grudgingly, Dominic nods. "You're right. Not letting him see her will only stir up more trouble. The old man can be stubborn as hell."

I try not to laugh at that. I'm thinking the apple didn't fall far from the tree.

"I guess we'll have to let him come—but *alone*," he says. "I'm not letting him bring his usual entourage with him. *Damn it!* I hate the idea of having him around you and Mia."

"Did you tell him her name?"

He nods. "I did. He said it was a fitting choice—that my mom would have loved it."

* * *

That night, after I nurse Mia, Dominic changes her diaper. I watch him, fascinated by his focus and attention to the slightest detail. My chest tightens, and my heart swells with love for this man. Physically, he's so intimidating, and yet he can be so incredibly gentle when the situation calls for it.

After he dresses her in a fresh sleeper, he lays her in the bassinet at the foot of our bed, and we head to the bathroom to get ready for bed ourselves. It's only ten o'clock, but we're both exhausted. And there's no telling how much sleep we'll get tonight. Mia might sleep for one hour or eight. Who knows?

Once we're in bed, I lie on my back in the semi-darkness. Dominic lies on his side facing me, gently tracing the curve of my cheek with his index finger. "You were amazing."

I smile. "I had a lot of help." I reach up and cup his face. "You were wonderful. I'm so proud of you."

"A few times I thought I was going to have a heart attack. I don't ever want to see you in discomfort like that again."

I grin at him. "Are you saying you don't want any more kids?"

"No!" He shakes his head emphatically. "I just don't like knowing you're hurting."

I stroke my thumb across his bearded cheek. "It never stopped my parents from having more kids. I have six siblings."

Dominic shakes his head. "Your poor dad. I don't know how he survived it." He leans close and presses his lips gently to mine. "I love you." His deep voice cracks when he says, "You and Mia are *everything* to me."

My throat tightens at the intensity of raw emotion in his voice. "I love you, too," I whisper back. "My rock."

When he leans down and kisses me again, I feel the dampness on his cheeks. My big strong man is a teddy bear. I smile, imagining Mia with her daddy wrapped around her little finger.

7

Dominic

Sophie drifts off to sleep pretty quickly, leaving me lying wide awake in our bed for hours as I battle my demons. First and foremost, I want to go beat the living daylights out of Cochran for daring to think he could keep Sophie like some kind of captive. The only thing keeping me from going after him right this minute is that he's cooling his heels behind bars.

Shane's attorney, Troy Spencer, called earlier in the evening to assure me there's no chance he'll get bail and that Cochran will stay in jail until the arraignment next week. He said the police had collected significant evidence, but he wasn't at liberty to say more at the time.

Part of me is tempted to tell Franco what Cochran did, because Sophie is now officially part of Franco Alessio's *family*, and no one hurts family. I'd have to make only one phone call, and Cochran wouldn't make it through the night. My father has connections all throughout the city. I doubt there's anywhere he couldn't reach if he felt motivated to do so. Even inside the county jail.

Just one damn phone call.

But I can't do it. I swore to myself that I'd never let my father's world touch Sophie or our family. And I know, no matter what Cochran did, Sophie would never approve of a hit job.

Sophie shifts beside me in bed and whimpers softly. I'm sure she's sore and every little movement is probably uncomfortable. I freeze as I listen to her breathing, trying to determine if she's awake or not. But I don't hear any more sounds, and her breathing remains steady and even. After a minute, I relax again.

Not long after, Mia makes a noise—a combination of a breathy cry and a squeak. I'm out of bed in an instant to check on her, but she quickly settles back to sleep with her tiny fist pressed against her mouth.

I sit on the side of the bed and watch my daughter sleep. How can anything possibly be so tiny and so perfect? I think she looks like Sophie. Sophie thinks she looks like my mom. My grandparents gave me a photo album filled with pictures of my mom from throughout her life—even pics of her when she started working for Franco, and then when she was pregnant with me. God, what a cliché! The mob boss gets his pretty, young housemaid pregnant.

Mia lets out a soft sigh, followed by a hiccup, and again I'm on high alert in case she wakes up and starts crying.

Sophie rolls over to face my side of the bed and reaches for me, but I'm not there. When her hand finds the mattress empty, she comes more fully awake, opens her eyes, and lifts her head. "Dominic?"

"I'm here, babe," I say quietly. "Just checking on Mia. She made a noise."

Sophie chuckles. "Babies make lots of noises, honey. It's okay. Is she still asleep?"

"Yeah."

She holds her hand out and sighs. "Come back to bed. I really need you to hold me right now."

She doesn't have to ask twice. I'm right back under

the covers in a heartbeat. Sophie rolls to her side, facing away from me, and I spoon her from behind. Her butt is tucked close to my groin, nestled tight and warm against my semi-hard erection. I'm tryin' real hard to be a gentleman here, but when she's this close to me, my body reacts. I can't help it.

I wrap my arm around her soft, round belly. She clutches my arm to her chest, and the tighter she holds onto me, the more my heart aches.

I've got two girls to take care of now—and for the moment, I'm not going to dwell on the shitty job I did of taking care of Sophie. We're going to have a talk about that—later. Not while she's recovering. And not while I'm still reeling from the events of the past forty-eight hours and the evidence the police have turned up.

He tried to take my wife and child.

I press my face into the back of Sophie's head and inhale deeply. Her scent calms me.

She's here. She's home. She's safe.

I think it'll be a good long while before I let her and Mia out of my sight—if ever. Certainly not before Cochran's behind bars for good.

That's the last thing I remember before sleep finally overtakes me.

***

Mia wakes up for real around three a.m., fussing in her bassinet. She's not crying exactly, but she's clearly unhappy.

"I should try to nurse her," Sophie says groggily as she pushes herself up to lean against the headboard. She gasps and winces as she settles.

I stuff a pillow behind her back, trying to make her more comfortable. "I'll get her."

"Would you please check her diaper?"

I unsnap her sleeper and reach inside to feel her diaper. "She's wet. How can such a little thing pee that much?"

Sophie laughs. "What goes in must come out."

I reach for the diaper bag. "I'll change her."

"Do you want help?"

"No. I got this." After I clean her up and put on a fresh diaper, I tuck her little legs back into her sleeper and snap it up. Little wisps of brown hair peek out from beneath her little baby hat. When she starts sucking on her fist, her lips smacking, I scoop her up. In my big paws, she seems even smaller.

I carry Mia to the bed. She's starting to squirm and

squeak. I kiss her forehead before I hand her off to Sophie. "Here's your mama, peanut."

I settle back into bed and watch in awe as Sophie nurses our daughter. I'm trying not to stare, but honestly, it's fascinating to see. Sophie was already well-endowed, but now, post pregnancy, her breasts are even bigger, fuller, rounder.

"My milk's really coming in," Sophie says, giving me a smile that melts my heart.

I can't look away. "Lucky baby," I mutter under my breath, and Sophie laughs.

* * *

Bridget comes over around eight the next morning to make us breakfast. Sophie settles on the sofa across the room, holding Mia, and watches her mom work in the kitchen.

Bridget cracks a bunch of eggs into a bowl. "Hannah and Killian are chomping at the bit to come over. Is it okay if I tell them they can come?"

Sophie's middle sister, Hannah, and her boyfriend, Killian Devereaux, flew in yesterday from Denver, Colorado. They're staying next door with Bridget and Calum.

"Sure," Sophie says. "They can come any time."

Bridget sends a quick text message to her middle daughter. "They're bringing a surprise with them," she says with a mysterious grin.

"What? The dog?" I know Hannah has a Belgian Malinois pup that she's training to do search and rescue in the Rockies.

"You'll see," Bridget says.

Twenty minutes later, we hear a knock on the front door. I get up to answer it. Not surprisingly, Hannah and Killian are standing on our front porch. The real surprise is that they're not alone. They brought my good buddy Owen Ramsey.

"Son of a—" But before I can get another word out, Owen steps forward and wraps me in a big bear hug.

"You sure are a sight for sore eyes," he says as he pounds my back. "Congratulations, man."

Owen and I go way back. We met years ago when we both served in the Marine Corps. When I first met Sophie and had to whisk her out of Chicago to protect her from a mob hit put out by my own father, I took her to my cabin in the Smoky Mountains in Tennessee. That was the safest place I could think of. And I knew with Owen nearby, living on the same mountain in his off-grid cabin, I could keep Sophie safe. Owen and Sophie became good friends in the process.

Owen now lives in Bryce, Colorado, with his wife, Maggie, who's expecting.

I invite them all in. Sophie lights up when she sees the new arrivals walk into the family room. "Oh, my god, you guys!"

Hannah rushes forward to hug her big sister. Then she scoops her brand-new niece into her arms, freeing Sophie to rise to her feet and hug Killian and Owen. "I can't believe this, Owen!" Sophie says. "It's so good to see you."

"It was a last-minute decision," Owen said. "But I had to come pay my respects and see the new baby. It's a short trip because I don't want to leave Maggie home alone for long. She insists on working at the store full time, even in her condition. I'll head back day after tomorrow."

Sophie reaches out to squeeze Owen's hand. "I'm so happy for you guys. When's she due?"

"Maggie's six months along," Owen says. "She wanted to come, but we decided it would be best for her to stay home."

Mia is soon passed around by our visitors. Killian looks far from comfortable holding a newborn, and Hannah doesn't waste an opportunity to tease him. "Don't worry. She's not going to break."

Killian frowns. "But she's so small." He passes Mia to Owen. "Here, you need the practice more than I do."

Owen cradles Mia to his chest, seeming pretty at ease with the whole process.

After everyone's had a turn to *ooh* and *ahh* over the baby, Sophie lays her down in the bassinet, and we all sit around the table to have breakfast.

Halfway through the meal, we hear a knock on the front door. Then it opens and in walks Lia—Sophie's youngest sister—and her husband, Jonah.

"Now all three of my girls are here," Bridget says as she grabs plates for the two newcomers.

Lia heads straight for the bassinet. "Where is she? Can I hold her?" She's already lifting the baby out.

Sophie laughs. "Of course you can."

Lia cuddles the baby close to her chest, then turns to her husband. "Look at this sweet face. And that little button nose!" Lia glances at Dominic and shakes her head. "How did a brute like you father such a delicate little baby girl?" She chuckles. "Don't worry, sweet pea. You look all sweet and innocent now, but Aunty Lia will teach you how to be a bad ass."

8

Sophie

After breakfast, everyone congregates in the family room. Mia is passed from person to person so the new arrivals have a chance to hold her. She mostly sleeps through it all.

The doorbell rings, and my dad jumps to his feet. "I'll get it." He returns a moment later with my brother Jamie and his fiancé, Molly. "Look who I found lurking outside."

Lots of hugging ensues. Afterward, Jamie says with

a grin, "We were just in the neighborhood and thought we'd stop by." Since they live twenty minutes away in Wicker Park, that's obviously not true.

Jamie takes off dark glasses and hooks them over the neckline of his shirt. As a result of a severe injury when he served in the Navy SEALS, he lost both eyes. He now has prosthetic eyes that are almost perfectly matched to the brown eyes he was born with. Since meeting him, Molly has helped him feel more comfortable going without the glasses. She says she likes seeing his eyes.

"When are you guys going to move here?" Mom asks. "There's plenty of room. You could build a house with an art studio for Molly."

"Actually, we're thinking about it," Jamie says.

Of all my siblings, my brothers Jamie and Liam are the only ones who haven't decided to build a house here in our family's private gated community. I can understand why Liam's not ready to move. He's young, and he likes living in the apartment building Shane owns. All the younger bodyguards live in that building, and they like being located close to each other. He and his girlfriend, Jasmine, would really miss living so close to their friends.

Molly holds Jamie's hand as she leads him to the sofa

where I'm sitting. Dominic rises to his feet and pats Jamie's shoulder. "Here, you can have my seat."

Jamie sits beside me, and Molly sits on his other side.

"Do you want to hold her?" I ask him.

Grinning. "You know I do."

"Lia," I call across the room to my youngest sister. "It's Uncle Jamie's turn to hold Mia."

Lia hands the baby to Jamie. "You need the practice more than I do, dude," she says as she winks at Molly.

Jamie and Molly are engaged to be married, and it's no secret that they're eager to have kids of their own.

Jamie settles Mia in the crook of his arm, and she relaxes into his hold. With the tip of his index finger, he gently traces her face… her brows, her forehead, her cheeks, her adorable little nose, her pouty rosebud lips. He strokes the soft downy fuzz on her head. "What color is her hair?"

"Brown," Dominic says. "The same color as Sophie's."

Molly reaches over and strokes Mia's hair. "It's a light chestnut brown with glints of red when the light hits it just right." Leave it to the artist to get descriptive when it comes to color.

Jamie smiles. His hair is auburn, a deep brown tinted with red. "Just like mine," he says with a smile. "How about her eyes?"

"Blue so far," I say. "But that could change." My chest tightens as I watch my brother holding my daughter. As a retired Navy SEAL, my brother is well trained in hand-to-hand combat. Despite his blindness, he's still quite capable of being lethal if the occasion calls for it. And yet, with my daughter, he's as gentle as a lamb.

I sneak a peek at Molly, whose attention is focused solely on Jamie and Mia. Her love for my brother is plain to see.

When Mia starts squirming and begins working her way up to a cry, Jamie rests her against his chest and pats her back. "What's wrong, little lady?"

"She's hungry," Dominic says. "If she's awake, she's hungry."

"Well, I can't help her there," Jamie says, chuckling as he hands her to me.

Dominic takes Mia from me and holds her in one arm while he gives me his other hand and helps me stand.

"If you'll excuse me," I say, "Mia needs her second breakfast."

The rest of the morning is filled with family. My sister-in-law Beth's mom, Ingrid, stops by to say hi and see Mia. She lives across the street from us. Jake, Annie, and their kids stop by to say hi. Beth, Shane, and their two kids make an appearance, along with Sam and Cooper. Liam and Jasmine drop by, too.

The whole family's here in one place at the same time. My parents sit on another sofa, my dad's arm across my mom's shoulders, with smiles on both of their faces.

* * *

Later that afternoon, after everyone leaves, Dominic suggests we go lie down for a bit. I could kiss the man because he's a mind reader. I'm absolutely wiped out. I love having family over, but right now my energy reserves are pretty low. Mom and Dad were the last ones to let themselves out, offering to come back later to help out with anything we need. We retire to our bedroom with Mia. She's ready to eat again, so I get comfy in bed, leaning against a small mound of pillows against the headboard and nurse her.

Dominic is beside me, watching in utter fascination. His phone vibrates and he picks it up to glance at the screen. I can tell instantly he's not happy. His expression tightens, and his lips flatten.

"Who is it?" I ask.

"My dad."

"Are you going to answer it?"

He shrugs. "I might as well. He'll just keep calling if I don't."

Dominic has a complicated relationship with his father. Franco Alessio is the head of a Chicago criminal enterprise—a mob to put it bluntly. Dominic is the son Franco fathered on a young housemaid, Mia Zaretti. Mia was cast out of the Alessio home by Franco's embittered wife, who was jealous of the attention her husband paid to the beautiful young woman. Franco loved Mia, but his wife threatened to have her killed if he didn't remove her from the household. He complied, knowing his wife was ruthless and perfectly capable of following through on her threat. After Dominic's mother passed away when he was ten, he was adopted by his maternal grandparents.

Dominic has never wanted to have anything to do with his crime boss father, but Franco has always been desperate to have a relationship with Dominic—his eldest son. Franco has another son, Mikey, with his wife. Mikey is currently serving time in a maximum-security federal prison for murdering a Chicago assistant district attorney. That's a long story for another time, but suffice it to say that's how Dominic and I met—when my brother Shane hired Dominic to protect me when Franco had ordered a hit on me so I wouldn't be able to testify in court against Mikey.

In the end, Dominic made a deal with his father to get Franco to call off the hit. In exchange for my safety, Dominic agreed to join his father's organization. But, when Franco learned I was carrying Dominic's child, he took pity on us and released Dominic from his agreement, allowing us to be together. Franco didn't want Dominic to lose his child the way he lost Dominic.

Dominic stares hard at his vibrating phone. I wait, watching silently while he decides his course of action. The phone goes silent, and we both sit quietly. Then the vibrating starts up again.

Dominic scowls. "I told you. He'll just keep calling." Sighing, he accepts the call. "What?" He listens for a couple of minutes, and then finally says, "Yes, you can come. But alone. No bodyguards, no muscle. You don't need them—this is a secured community." Dominic listens a little while longer, then ends the call. "He agreed to my terms."

"When's he coming?"

"This evening at seven." With an exasperated growl, Dominic climbs off the bed and starts pacing. I watch silently, biting my tongue, as he runs his fingers through his hair. This is something he has to come to grips with on his own.

He returns to the bed just as Mia falls asleep. "Here, I'll take her." He gazes down at her, studying her features, her tiny hands, her little feet. "She'll be tall, won't she?"

I nod. "Probably. With us for parents, how could she not?"

He nods. "That's good. I want her to be tall. And Lia wasn't too far off the mark. When Mia's older, we need to make sure she can protect herself. Martial arts training wouldn't be a bad idea." He gives me a wry look. "Maybe for you, too."

I run my hand down his back. "You're going to be such a wonderful father."

He scoffs. "Hell, Phee, I have no idea what I'm doing. I don't know how to be a dad."

I laugh quietly. "Yes, you do. You've observed my brothers with their kids."

"Yeah, well, you McIntyres are naturals when it comes to children. You all have the parenting gene. Me? No. When I was growing up, I never saw my dad. The only thing I knew about him was that he was a criminal. I have no experience to go by."

I slide my hand down to Dominic's thigh. "You have nothing to worry about. Look at you cuddling with her. You're a natural, too."

He chuckles. "No. I'm just being careful not to bruise her, that's all. My number one rule—don't hurt the baby. The rest I'm making up as I go."

"All right, *Daddy.* Why don't you check her diaper and put her in her bassinet? Then we can all take naps."

Dominic climbs out of bed, carefully clutching Mia to his chest as he walks to the foot of our bed—as if there's even a remote chance he would drop her. He lays her in the bassinet, unsnaps her sleeper, then glances up at me. "She's dry."

"Wonderful." I hold out my arms. "Then come back to bed and cuddle with *me.*"

"That's a given," he says with a grin. He comes back to bed and takes me in his arms, and we lie on our sides, facing each other.

Dominic brushes back my hair. "You are amazing." He presses his lips to mine, his kiss gentle and unhurried. "My beautiful wife." Another kiss. "Mother of my child." Another kiss, this time on my cheek. "My goddess." Another kiss, on my forehead. "My best friend." Then his mouth drifts back down to capture mine.

I smile against his lips. "I think you're a little biased."

"I'm not. I'm being completely objective." He threads his fingers through my hair, sliding his hand behind my head to grasp the back of my neck. "I want to be a good husband and a good father, and I'm counting on you to teach me how."

Dominic pulls me into his arms, and I sigh as I rest my head against his broad chest. Now that Mia's safely here and we're all home, I finally have time to think about what Gordon did. The man's always been eccentric, but I never dreamed he could do anything as crazy as trying to hold me captive. Dominic has said very little about it since he rescued me. I think he's trying to shield me.

"What's going to happen to Gordon?" I ask.

Dominic tenses. "It's being handled, babe. You don't need to worry about it."

I lift my head and level my gaze at him. "The man kidnapped me, Dominic. I think I have the right to know what's being done about it."

"I told you, he's cooling his heels in the county jail until arraignment."

"And then?"

He shrugs. "The evidence the police have collected already is overwhelming. He's going to be charged with a long list of crimes, and he's going to spend a long time in prison."

"Unless he's found mentally incompetent to stand trial. What man in his right mind would do something so crazy?"

Dominic grunts.

"It's possible, you know," I say. "He's not in his right mind. It wouldn't take much to convince a judge that he's not mentally competent."

"Then he'll be locked up in a psychiatric hospital. Either way, he's not getting out for a very long time. I promise you, Mia will be an adult before Cochran is released." He tightens his hold on me. "I'm tryin' real hard not to think about what could have happened if I hadn't found you when I did." He shudders. "I'm also tryin' real hard not to go off him myself."

"Don't even joke about that. You can't. Let the system work. Let the DA's office handle Gordon."

"I'll tell you one thing, babe. I'm putting my foot down right now. You are *never* to go alone to a client's home, ever again. Is that clear?"

I press my lips together to stifle a laugh. "Yes, dear."

He gently smacks my behind. "I'm serious, Phee. It's not a laughing matter. This could have turned out really bad."

"But it didn't. I knew you'd find me, Dominic. I never doubted it. Not for a second."

9

Dominic

Exactly at seven p.m., there's a knock on our front door. "He's here," I say to Sophie. "At least he's punctual." We're lounging on the sofa watching one of her favorite decorating shows on TV.

Of course, I already knew he was here. The security guard at the front gate notified me of Franco's arrival. Franco passed through the gate alone, as requested. His personal protection squad remained outside the gate.

I open the front door to my father, who's standing

there in a black suit and tie, white dress shirt, holding a bouquet of long-stemmed roses and a little pink gift bag. And I do mean *little*. It's not even big enough to hold a donut, for fuck's sake. I'm afraid to ask what's in there.

Franco is a big man, like me. Obviously, he's where I got my height. His hair is far darker than mine, nearly black, except for the liberal amount of gray strands at his temples. In fact, I think he's gone even more gray since the last time I saw him. His features are stern, as is his expression.

Suddenly, his eyes soften and he smiles. "Congratulations on the birth of your daughter, my son. I'm very happy for you."

Nodding, I step back so Franco can enter.

"You're looking well," he says in his deep voice.

"Other than being exhausted, I'm fine." I nod toward the great room. "This way."

Franco follows me to the back of the house, where we find Sophie sitting upright on the sofa. Mia is asleep in a pumpkin seat on the coffee table.

Sophie starts to rise, but Franco holds out his hand. "No, dear. Don't get up on my account. Sit and be comfortable."

"Hello, Mr. Alessio," Sophie says, offering him a hesitant smile. "We're so glad you came."

"Please, call me Franco," he says. "Or you may call me *dad*." Franco tosses me a wry glance, most likely because I refuse to call him that.

Sophie bites her lip to keep from smiling. Of course she gets his meaning. "Franco," she says.

Franco hands her the bouquet of roses, along with the tiny pink gift bag. "That's for the little lady."

I take the flowers from Sophie to free her hands and carry them to the kitchen. Sophie keeps a collection of glass vases in a cupboard, so I grab one, fill it with water, and stuff the roses inside.

From across the room, I hear Franco say, "Go ahead and open it," to Sophie.

I rejoin them as Sophie opens the little bag and peers inside. She pulls out a small slip of paper and unfolds it. Her eyes go wide as she glances up at me.

She hands it to me, and I stare at the check made out to Mia Olivia Zaretti, for one million dollars, signed by Franco Alessio. *Holy shit.* "Franco—"

"It's for her dowry," he replies.

I grit my teeth in an effort to remain calm. "Our daughter doesn't need a dowry." I try to hand the check back, but he refuses. "Take it, Franco. She doesn't need it. Sophie and I—"

"I know you can provide for your daughter. I didn't mean to imply otherwise. This is for *her*, when she's an adult. A little something from her grandfather to help her get a start in life."

I sigh heavily. "I need a drink." I cross the room to the wet bar and pour myself a shot of whiskey, neat.

Franco appears beside me. "Aren't you going to offer your old man a drink?"

I pour him one and set it on the bar. He takes it, and we both knock back our shots.

My chest tightens painfully. *I'm having a drink with my dad.*

"The money wasn't meant as an insult," he says in a low voice. "I just wanted to give my granddaughter something nice. I have nothing else to offer her, other than money."

I chuckle. "A stuffed animal would have been *nice*. A pair of pink booties would have been *nice*. A million dollars? That's something entirely different."

"Well, get over it, son, because I'm not taking the money back. It belongs to Mia. Consider it a downpayment on her inheritance."

A downpayment?

I glance across the room at Sophie, who's taking Mia out of the pumpkin seat.

Sophie straightens, holding our daughter, who's wrapped in a pale yellow blanket, in her arms. "Would you like to hold your granddaughter?" she asks Franco.

Franco gives me a triumphant look. "I'd love to."

* * *

"It was a nice visit, except for the check," Sophie says as we get ready for bed that night. Mia's been fed and is already fast asleep in her bassinet. Sophie and I are standing at the his-and-hers bathroom sinks, brushing our teeth. "What do we do about the money?"

"What do you want to do?" I ask her as I'm brushing my teeth. "We can always give the check back to Franco, or just tear it up."

She shrugs. "I don't think we have the right to make that decision for Mia. She can decide for herself when she's an adult. For now, I think we should deposit the money into an investment account. It's her money, Dominic. By the time she's an adult, her portfolio will be significant."

I rinse my brush and nod. "All right."

I can't help admiring Sophie's reflection in the bathroom mirror. Her long, wavy hair is freshly brushed and hanging loose past her shoulders. She looks happy and relaxed, her cheeks a bit flushed. She's wearing a pale blue silk nightgown—one specially designed for nursing mothers. It's got a bra built into it, and the cups unsnap for easy access. Her figure is soft and lush, her breasts large. I'm trying not to stare, but damn, it's hard.

After I rinse out the toothpaste and wipe my mouth, I step behind her and wrap my arms around her, resting them just under her breasts. I feel like a heel when all of a sudden I get a hard-on. I know she can feel it prodding her backside.

She catches my gaze in the mirror and smiles. "Sorry, pal."

I grin guiltily. "I can't help it. I take one look at you, and I get hard. My dick doesn't understand that you just gave birth."

She gives me a devilish grin.

Done brushing, she wipes her mouth on a tissue and turns in my arms to face me. "I love you."

"My beautiful Phee." My hands slide down to cup her lush ass, and my pulse starts pounding. "It's gonna be a long six weeks."

She laughs. "Don't worry. I have two hands and a mouth."

I scoop her up into my arms and carry her to our bed. "Don't tease me, woman. My heart can't take it."

* * *

The next few days are quiet ones. Sophie and I spend a lot of time in bed, relaxing, staring in awe at our daughter and wondering how in the world we managed to create something so perfect.

Later in the week, our peace is shattered when Shane calls to warn me that he and Troy and Tyler Jamison—Shane's brother-in-law and a former police detective—are coming over. "We need to talk, Dominic."

That can't be good. "Sure. Come on over."

When they arrive, I escort them into the home office at the front of the house—far away from where Sophie is in the kitchen.

"All right, spill it," I say. I'm leaning against the mahogany desk. Shane, Troy, and Tyler are all standing, facing me. I can tell by their expressions that they don't like what they're about to tell me.

"First things first," Troy says. Mr. Armani is dressed

in a black suit and tie, looking very much like the corporate attorney he is. He's the main attorney for McIntyre Security. He's also Shane's friend and personal attorney. Troy sets his briefcase down on the floor. "The police need to talk to Sophie. They've been very patient, respecting her recent delivery, but it's time. They have questions for her. They need her to make a statement."

Reluctantly, I nod. I knew this was coming. "All right. Fine. What else. You guys didn't come all this way just to tell me that."

Tyler speaks up. "As you know, Cochran's assistant, Marcus Lane, was apprehended at a local private airfield. The man's a licensed pilot. He was prepping Cochran's private jet for an international flight."

My heart stills. "And?" I know the other shoe is about to drop.

Tyler continues. "A great deal of evidence was collected from the airplane, including suitcases containing women's clothing, as well as baby items—clothes, diapers, and so on."

My stomach hollows out, and I feel sick. "I need to sit down," I say as I walk around to the other side of the desk and sit in the black leather chair. "Go on."

"But that's not all," Tyler says. "They found a passport

for an adult woman named *Sophie Cochran,* as well as one for an infant girl named *Amelia Cochran.*"

"He planned this well in advance," Shane says, his expression tight. "He even knew Sophie was having a girl."

That son-of-a-bitch was attempting to take my wife and daughter out of the country. "Where was he planning to take them?"

"Earlier in the day, Lane filed a flight plan to Indonesia," Tyler says. "The authorities in Indonesia have confirmed that Cochran owns a large estate on one of the country's most remote islands."

I sit in the desk chair, numb. I'm finding it hard to even process this. I look up at the three of them. "Please tell me he'll never get out of prison."

Troy nods. "Based on the evidence that's been collected so far, I don't think he'll ever get out."

I look to Shane. "I need to take a leave of absence from work. I'm sticking close to Sophie and the baby until the legal proceedings are over and Cochran's locked up. Even then, I might not come back to work."

Shane nods. "Do whatever you need to do, but Dominic—this wasn't your fault."

I shake my head, but don't bother arguing with him. Right now my mind is reeling after hearing what Cochran had planned, and my gut tells me to never let Sophie out of my sight again.

After the guys leave, I go in search of my wife. I find her in our bedroom changing Mia's diaper. Without saying a word, I walk up behind her, slip my arms around her, and press my lips to the back of her head. I can't help thinking about what could have happened.

She turns to face me. "What's wrong?"

I realize my arms are shaking, and that gave me away. How do I tell her this? How do I tell her what that psycho was planning to do with her and our child?

"What did they want?" she asks.

I start with the easy part. "The police are coming by tomorrow at two o'clock to interview you. They need an official statement."

She nods, watching me warily. "Okay. That's fine. What else? What are you not telling me?"

I sit her down on the bed, take her hands in mine, and repeat everything Shane and the guys shared with me about Cochran's presumed plans. When I'm done, she's as white as a ghost, seemingly in shock.

"I promise you, Phee, no matter what it takes—Cochran will *never* be in a position to hurt you or Mia again."

She stares at me with wide blue eyes as her brain attempts to process what I've told her.

I squeeze her chilled hands. "Babe? Do you hear what I'm saying?" She knows as well as I do that one call to Franco would neutralize the threat for good.

Slowly, she nods.

When her tears start, I pull her to me and wrap my arms around her. Now she's the one shaking. "I will never let anything happen to you and Mia, I swear," I say.

And that's a vow I intend to keep.

Epilogue

Sophie
Two Months Later

Today marks the end of my maternity leave from my interior design business. I start back to work on Monday. Only this time, things are going to be a bit different. Even though Gordon Cochran pled guilty to a laundry list of kidnapping and related charges, he hasn't been sentenced yet. Troy Spencer assures us he'll get at least twenty years, if not more, in a federal prison. He tried to kidnap *two* people, not just one, so that doubles the penalty.

Despite Gordon pleading guilty, Dominic is still on

high alert and as vigilant as ever. His temporary absence from McIntyre Security turned into a resignation. He's now going to be working with me on a full-time basis in a security capacity. Technically, he's not my bodyguard, but for all intents and purposes, he might as well be. It's a good thing I'm head over heels in love with him, or he'd drive me crazy.

At Dominic's request, I've hired two more designers to help me run my business, allowing me to cut my hours to part time. I'm planning to work out of our home office a couple of days a week. I think I'm going to like this slower change of pace because it will allow me to be with Mia all the time. When we do go into the office, she'll be coming with us. I asked Alison to turn one of our small conference rooms into a nursery, and she was thrilled to be given that project. I can't wait to see the end result.

"Ready?" I ask Dominic, who's putting Mia in a lightweight spring jacket.

He lifts her up into the air in front of him and gives her a big smile. "Are you ready to go visit your auntie and uncle and cousins?" Then he slips her into the baby carrier strapped to his broad chest.

Today's a big day. My brother Shane and his family are moving into their new home, which is located next door to ours. Their best friends, Sam and Cooper, are moving in with them. It just makes sense as Sam is Beth's full-time bodyguard. The two couples had an architect design a two-family home for them, so while both families have their own private space, there's a lot of shared space, too—a large gourmet kitchen, dining room, great room, laundry room, home theater, and gym.

The moving truck arrived a short while ago, and their furniture is being unloaded now.

By the time we show up, the front yard of their house is nothing short of a circus. Mom and Dad are here, as are Annie and her three kids. And now us.

Aiden runs up to Dominic and raises his arms. "Uncle Dominic! Can I sit on your shoulders?"

"Sure," Dominic says as he removes Mia from the baby carrier strapped to his chest and hands her to me. Then he lifts Aiden high overhead to sit on his shoulders.

Aiden raises his arms into the air. "You're even bigger than my dad!"

Beth and Sam and Cooper pull up in Cooper's black Escalade. Sam helps Beth wrangle the kids—Ava in a stroller, Luke in Sam's arms. Cooper goes inside the house to help Shane with directing where all the furniture goes.

"Are you excited?" I ask Beth as she hands Ava a stuffed animal to hold.

Beth looks a bit harried. "Yes and no. I'm excited about the new house, but I'm going to miss the penthouse. We have so much history there, you know? It's hard to say goodbye to it, but Luke really needs to be able to play outside and run around with his cousins. And it won't be long before Ava's running around, too.

"Hey, peeps!" Lia says as she walks across the street to join us.

Jonah's with her, and they're holding hands. So adorable.

"So, today's the big day," she says to Beth. "I never thought you guys would get here." When Ava sees Lia, she raises her arms. Lia picks her up out of her stroller and props her on her hip. "Wow, with you guys moving in, our population here in the compound just went up by six."

Mom pats Lia's back. "Honey, please don't call it a compound. You make it sound like it's a prison."

"What do you want me to call it then?" Lia asks, laughing. "McIntyreland?"

Aiden asks to get down from Dominic's shoulders so he can play with his cousin Luke. The two boys are inseparable. Sam sets Luke on his feet and watches the two boys closely to make sure they don't get in the way of the movers.

"Now we just need to get Jamie and Molly here," Mom says. "Then most of my kids will be close."

We stand around watching the movers unload the furniture until lunch time comes around. The littlest ones are starting to get cranky, including Mia, who's due for a feeding.

"Why don't we take all the kids back to my house?" Mom asks. "I'll fix everyone some lunch."

All the kids and women walk over to my parents' house, along with Dominic, Jonah, and Sam.

Dominic tugs me aside when we reach our destination, letting everyone else file inside. He takes Mia from me. "Here, I'll hold her." Then he leans down and kisses me. "Do you know how much I love you?"

I smile. "I think so."

"Do you, really?"

"Probably." I'm sure I have a stupid grin on my face now.

He shakes his head. "I don't think you do." After kissing me once more, he says, "I guess I'll just have to show you when we get back home."

The heat in his eyes makes my belly quiver and my sex tingle.

Dominic opens the door for me, and we step inside the house. The kids are all seated at the kitchen table, and Mom, Beth, and Annie are making them peanut butter and jelly sandwiches.

Lia walks up to us and snatches Mia from Dominic's arms. "My turn," she says.

Dominic and I stand just inside the door, holding hands, and now we *both* have stupid smiles on our faces.

I sigh. "Everything's perfect, isn't it?"

Dominic nods. "Yes, it is."

* * *

Thank you for reading *Vanished*. I hope you enjoyed this follow-up to Sophie and Dominic's story. Stay tuned for more books in the *McIntyre Security Bodyguard* series.

* * *

If you'd like to receive free bonus content each month—exclusive for my newsletter subscribers—sign up for my newsletter on my website. You can also find links to my free short stories, information on upcom-

ing releases, a reading order, and more.
www.aprilwilsonauthor.com

* * *

Here are links to my list of audiobooks:
www.aprilwilsonauthor.com/audiobooks

* * *

I interact daily with readers in my Facebook reader group (April Wilson Reader Group) where I post frequent updates and share teasers. Come join me!

* * *

Books by April Wilson

McIntyre Security Bodyguard Series:

Vulnerable

Fearless

Shane–a novella

Broken

Shattered

Imperfect

Ruined

Hostage

Redeemed

Marry Me–a novella

Snowbound–a novella

Regret

With This Ring–a novella

Collateral Damage

Special Delivery

Vanished

McIntyre Security Bodyguard Series Box Sets:

Box Set 1

Box Set 2

Box Set 3

Box Set 4

McIntyre Security Protectors:
Finding Layla
Damaged Goods
Freeing Ruby

McIntyre Search and Rescue:
Search and Rescue
Lost and Found
Tattered and Torn

Tyler Jamison Novels:
Somebody to Love
Somebody to Hold
Somebody to Cherish

A British Billionaire Romance Series:
Charmed
Captivated

Miscellaneous Books:
Falling for His Bodyguard

* * *

Audiobooks by April Wilson
For links to my audiobooks, please visit my website:
www.aprilwilsonauthor.com/audiobooks

Made in the USA
Monee, IL
12 April 2023